Jessica pulled out her notebook. But instead of taking French notes, she wrote, *"So tell me, Jonathan Cain, do you always ignore damsels in distress, or were you just feeling rude yesterday?"*

Grinning mischievously, she ripped the page out and folded it in half. When Ms. Dalton's back was turned, she tossed it onto Jonathan's desk.

At first he ignored the note. Jessica tapped her fingernails on her book, waiting. Finally he picked it up and unfolded it. Jessica's heart beat rapidly as she watched him reading. Then he quickly wrote something in the space below her message and returned the note to her desk.

Jessica's hands trembled as she read his response. *You don't want to mess with me,* it said. *I eat little girls like you for breakfast.*

TALL, DARK, AND DEADLY

Written by
Kate William

Created by
FRANCINE PASCAL

BANTAM BOOKS
NEW YORK · TORONTO · LONDON · SYDNEY · AUCKLAND

TALL, DARK, AND DEADLY
A BANTAM BOOK : 0 553 50456 8

Originally published in USA by Bantam Books

First publication in Great Britain

PRINTING HISTORY
Bantam edition published 1996

The trademarks "Sweet Valley" and "Sweet Valley High"
are owned by Francine Pascal and are used under license by
Bantam Books and Transworld Publishers Ltd.

Conceived by Francine Pascal

Produced by Daniel Weiss Associates, Inc,
33 West 17th Street, New York, NY 10011

Bantam Books are published by Transworld Publishers Ltd,
61–63 Uxbridge Road, Ealing, London W5 5SA,
in Australia by Transworld Publishers (Australia) Pty Ltd,
15–25 Helles Avenue, Moorebank, NSW 2170,
and in New Zealand by Transworld Publishers (NZ) Ltd,
3 William Pickering Drive, Albany, Auckland.

Printed and bound in Great Britain by
Cox & Wyman Ltd, Reading, Berkshire.

To Jenevieve Terese Campo

Chapter 1

"I can't believe there's not one interesting guy in here tonight," Jessica Wakefield complained as she scanned the crowd in the Dairi Burger, Sweet Valley's most popular hangout. The place was lively with the sounds of cheerful conversation and music from the jukebox, but every face was familiar—and boring. They were the same people Jessica saw every day at school. "Sweet Valley High is the *pits* when it comes to decent guys," she declared with a sigh.

A chorus of agreement sounded from the other girls in the booth. Sitting next to Jessica, Sandra Bacon flipped back her short dark blond hair and laughed derisively. "That explains why five of the most popular girls at Sweet Valley High are packed into this booth, chowing down

1

on burgers and shakes on a Saturday night."

Annie Whitman nodded emphatically. "It's so frustrating," she agreed, rolling her green eyes. "The good-looking guys are conceited; the charming guys are boring; the rich ones are complete jerks."

"And then you have Bruce Patman, who's rich, conceited, *and* a complete jerk," Jessica said, pointing to a nearby table where Bruce was apparently winning an arm-wrestling match. "It's so unfair for someone like him to be so rich," she muttered, thinking aloud. Bruce came from one of the wealthiest families in Sweet Valley, and although she had dated him in the past, Jessica considered him hopeless.

Lila Fowler sighed contentedly. "I'm so lucky. But I know exactly what you girls are going through."

Jessica braced herself. *Here we go again!* she thought, recognizing the sappy, faraway look in her best friend's brown eyes.

"Before I met Bo at Camp Echo Mountain," Lila began, "I used to think that a girl had to choose between looks, class, and personality when it came to guys. But Bo has it all. And he's so intelligent and sophisticated. He knows the names of all the constellations in the sky and speaks French, Italian, and German fluently. I just wish he didn't live in Washington, D.C. I miss him dreadfully."

Jessica rolled her eyes and yawned dramatically. She knew the gushing could go on for hours. The previous summer Jessica and her identical twin, Elizabeth, along with Lila and several other students from Sweet Valley High, had worked as junior counselors at Camp Echo Mountain, a performing-arts camp in Montana. Lila had fallen in love with Bo at first sight and had been driving Jessica crazy rhapsodizing about him ever since.

"And he's so gorgeous," Lila continued. "He has this adorable crooked smile, and did I mention that he has impeccable taste? He can tell the difference between beluga caviar and the cheaper kinds that come from whitefish and herring. He's traveled all over the world. . . ."

Jessica smiled as her thoughts drifted to her own camp romance with Paul Mathis, a gorgeous guy who lived near Camp Echo Mountain. They hadn't made any promises to each other, but after all they'd shared, Jessica knew she'd always have a special place in her heart for Paul. *He'll never forget me either,* she told herself. *How could he?*

An excited cheer came from Bruce's table. Amy Sutton rolled her eyes. "I wish you could just

3

date a guy's *car*," she said wistfully, referring to the sleek black Porsche Bruce drove.

The other girls laughed. "That's an interesting idea," Sandy remarked.

Lila shook her head pensively. "Bruce's problem is clearly *amour propre*."

Jessica shrieked, "*Please!* No French phrases. We're *eating*."

Lila glared at Jessica with a look of indignation. "OK, fine. Love of self, then. Vanity. You don't have to get rude about it, Jessica."

Jessica laughed. "Don't knock my rudeness, Lila. In a minute I'm going to pelt you with greasy french fries."

Lila batted her eyelashes, giving Jessica a withering, condescending look. "I see you've learned a lot from your experience at Camp Echo Mountain," she replied. "You must have been paying close attention during the food fights in the mess hall."

Amy spooned a glob of ice cream dripping with fudge sauce into her mouth and dabbed her lips with the corner of a paper napkin. "And then there's Ken Matthews," she commented.

Jessica frowned. "What about him?"

Amy licked the spoon, then swirled it absently across the top of her sundae. "Ken was the last decent guy at Sweet Valley High. But he's got such a bad attitude now, ever since you cheated on him."

4

Jessica glared at Amy. An awkward, tense silence fell over the booth. "I had my reasons," Jessica said. "And besides, it's ancient history."

Amy shrugged. "I'm just saying that Ken is different now, that's all."

Jessica shifted uncomfortably in her seat. Thinking of her horrible breakup with Ken Matthews, the captain of the Sweet Valley High football team, brought back a flood of painful memories. She pushed them to a far corner of her mind and quickly changed the subject. "Look what my grandmother sent me," she said brightly, showing off the diamond studs in her ears. "She sent Elizabeth a pair too."

"They're beautiful," Sandy declared. The others murmured in agreement.

Jessica took out one of the earrings and passed it around the table. "My grandmother's cool," she said. "When she was twelve, she was the first girl in her town to get her ears pierced."

"They're gorgeous," Annie breathed as she placed the earring in Amy's outstretched palm.

"Oh, wow! It's so sparkly," Amy exclaimed, holding it up to the light. She passed it to Lila.

"This looks like a very good quality diamond," Lila proclaimed, examining it closely before giving it back to Jessica. "And the setting is exquisite," she added.

"They have a lot of sentimental value too," Jessica said as she slipped the gold post back into her ear. "I don't get to see my grandmother very often, and these will remind me of her."

They were interrupted by the sound of a loud crash, followed by hoots of male laughter. A waitress had dropped a platter of food, which the guys at Bruce's table seemed to find hilariously funny. Jessica shook her head in dismay as she watched the red-faced woman stoop to pick up the mess.

"Even if they weren't diamonds, I think Jessica's earrings have more sentimental value than all the guys in here combined," Sandy declared.

Elizabeth hummed along with the radio as she flipped through the contents of her closet, trying to decide what to wear that evening. She studied her sleeveless pale blue cotton dress for a moment, then pushed it aside and pulled out the next item in line, a peach-colored knitted tunic.

Holding the tunic under her chin, she turned toward the mirror above her dresser and looked at her reflection. The shirt was fine, and her new diamond earrings were gorgeous. But the blue-green eyes that stared back at her seemed cloudy and anxious. Elizabeth mentally kicked herself. *Snap out of it!* she ordered herself.

She and her longtime boyfriend, Todd Wilkins, were planning a romantic picnic on the beach that evening. She had a basket ready in the kitchen, packed with cheese, warm bread, juicy pears, and homemade pecan cookies. "It's going to be wonderful, and I can't wait," she said to her reflection in the mirror. But her voice sounded unconvincing, even to her own ears.

Elizabeth sighed deeply and returned the tunic to her closet. *Why is everything I own so bland?* she wondered, frustrated. She considered raiding Jessica's closet, where she was sure to find bright colors and trendy fashions. But Elizabeth knew it wasn't just the clothes. *My whole life is bland!* she realized.

"But this is who I am," she said softly, admitting the truth. The pastels and natural tones of her wardrobe suited her lifestyle, which was serious, quiet, and well ordered. And no matter how confused and out-of-sorts she felt, Elizabeth wouldn't want to change places with her twin.

She and Jessica were as different as two sixteen-year-old girls could possibly be, in spite of being identical twins. Beyond their matching silky blond hair, blue-green eyes, and lean, athletic figures, the Wakefield twins were as similar as hot pink and light beige. Jessica lived for the moment and for taking advantage of all the

7

excitement and adventure that every moment could possibly offer. The twins were juniors at Sweet Valley High, but for Jessica, school was a place to gossip, check out guys, and pursue the only school activity she cared about—cheerleading.

Elizabeth was the older twin—by four minutes. But those minutes seemed to have made an enormous difference in their personalities. Unlike Jessica, Elizabeth carefully considered the consequences of her actions. She was a conscientious student and worked hard to earn high grades in all her classes. She also wrote a regular column called "Personal Profiles" for the *Oracle*, Sweet Valley High's school paper, and she hoped to become a professional writer someday.

When she wasn't studying or writing, Elizabeth enjoyed having fun just as much as Jessica did. But for Elizabeth, fun meant watching old movies, reading poetry, and hanging out with her small circle of friends. *And quiet, romantic dates with Todd*, she reminded herself pointedly.

But something was different lately. *Who am I?* she demanded of herself. Her clothes, her life—nothing seemed to fit anymore.

Feeling defeated, Elizabeth lowered her head. She knew exactly what the problem was: a letter she'd received that afternoon, one that felt as if it were burning a hole in the pocket of her jeans.

Elizabeth took out the peach tunic and carried it over to her bed. *What am I going to do?* she wondered as she paced across the room.

Exhaling deeply, she pulled out the letter and ran her fingers over the familiar white personalized stationery. Her name and address were written across the envelope in black ink, in a bold, angular script.

Her hands trembled as she took the letter out of the envelope and unfolded its pristine white pages. Unable to stop herself, she read it again, her heart beating rapidly.

Jessica and her friends were the last customers left in the Dairi Burger. "I think they're getting ready to close," Sandy said, jerking her thumb at the guy mopping the floor on the other side of the dining room.

"Is it that late already?" Annie asked incredulously.

Jessica looked at the pile of debris strewn across their table and giggled. "I'd say this has been quite the party, girls."

"Yeah," Annie agreed as she tossed her crumpled napkin onto one of the trays. "Who needs guys, anyway?"

Amy shrugged. "It would be nice to let them

9

pay the tab." The others groaned in unison.

Sandy picked up the wrappers in front of her and stuffed them into a paper cup. "I can't believe I drank two chocolate milkshakes tonight."

"Don't worry," Jessica assured with a laugh. "You'll burn up those extra calories during cheerleading practice next week. I came up with three new routines for the squad that will knock the fans right out of the bleachers." Jessica shared the SVH cheerleading captain position with Heather Mallone, who had been trying to outdo Jessica ever since she'd first arrived at Sweet Valley High. Their intense rivalry helped keep Jessica inspired.

Lila was the only one in the group who wasn't a member of the SVH cheerleading squad. "I'm thinking of working out with weights," she announced. "Bo says that free weights are the fastest way to get in shape. And you should see the muscles on him—washboard abs and iron shoulders . . ."

Jessica snorted. "Careful, Li. You don't want to start drooling all over your silk blouse."

Lila picked up her tray and scowled at Jessica. The girls continued chatting as they cleared off the table and dumped out their garbage.

Annie's silver Ford and Lila's green Triumph were the only cars left in the front parking lot. The girls parted company, and Lila and Jessica headed toward Lila's car.

"I wonder if Bo is going to send me more flowers this week," Lila remarked as she unlocked the doors of the Triumph. "My bedroom already looks like a flower shop."

Jessica hopped into the car and pulled the seat belt across her shoulder. "I'm thrilled for you, Lila," she said sarcastically.

Jessica had to admit that Bo Creighton was an OK guy—a bit snobbish maybe, but cute. But, above all, he and Lila were perfect for each other. They both came from wealthy families and they both hated roughing it. They'd spent most of their time at Camp Echo Mountain shopping by mail order for gourmet food and luxury items, using their credit cards. Bo had gotten in trouble with the director of Camp Echo Mountain for hiring the other guys in his cabin to do his chores.

Jessica had nothing against him personally, but after having listened to Lila gush about him endlessly, she wanted to scream every time she heard Bo's name.

Lila started the engine and glanced at Jessica. "Did I tell you that Bo sent me *The Collected Stories of Guy de Maupassant*?"

Jessica flashed her a wild look. "Yes, you did," she choked. "Seven times!"

"In a leather-bound, deluxe edition?" Lila asked. "Help!"

Lila giggled. "But did I tell you that Bo has read all of them in the original French version?"

"Yes!" Jessica shrieked. "At least twice. You're my best friend, Lila. Don't force me to strangle you." Lila glared at her in mock horror, and the two of them dissolved in a fit of laughter.

Suddenly Lila stopped laughing and gaped at Jessica with a wide-eyed look of shock.

Jessica frowned. "What's wrong?"

Lila made a breathy, wheezing sound and pointed at Jessica's ear. "It's gone."

"What are you talking about?" Jessica grumbled as she adjusted the rearview mirror with a hard yank. She looked at her reflection and gasped. One of her diamond earrings was missing. Jessica's heart plummeted. "This is horrible!" she cried. "It must have fallen out at the table." Lila nodded solemnly.

"Come on," Jessica said, pulling off her seat belt. "We can't leave until we find my earring." She pushed open the passenger-side door and jumped out of the car. Without waiting for Lila, Jessica went tearing back into the Dairi Burger.

Chapter 2

Elizabeth and Todd walked hand in hand along the dock at the Sweet Valley Marina, their footsteps echoing on the wooden planks. A salty breeze brushed across Elizabeth's face. In the sky, a brilliant half-moon hung over the horizon, shooting a streak of silver onto the surface of the dark, shimmering ocean. The waves splashed rhythmically against the dock. The boats bobbed and swayed in time. The setting couldn't have been more beautiful or more romantic. At that late hour, she and Todd had the entire place to themselves.

Todd hugged her close to his side, and Elizabeth rested her head on his shoulder. But in her heart, she knew there was something wrong.

Something is missing, an irritating voice in her head taunted. She squeezed her eyes shut, trying to block it out as she wrapped her arms around Todd's lean waist.

He lowered his lips to Elizabeth's and kissed her passionately. *I love Todd,* she thought.

When the kiss was over, he continued to hold her close, running his hand along her back. *This is wonderful,* Elizabeth forced herself to think. Todd kissed her neck, the side of her face, her forehead. *I love him, I love him, I love him,* she chanted in her mind.

But the moon over the water brought back memories of another place and time. Try as she might, Elizabeth couldn't keep the unwanted images away. Her imagination could easily turn the Pacific Ocean into a kidney-shaped lake, with mountain peaks looming in the horizon. Without any effort, she could almost smell the tangy fragrance of pine trees and the pungent smoke of campfires.

Other details came rushing back . . . late night canoe rides on a moonlit lake . . . passionate kisses in the woods behind the boathouse . . .

"I have a great idea," Todd whispered close to her ear.

Elizabeth's eyelids fluttered open. She blinked hard and gazed into his eyes. For an instant she felt confused, expecting to see a pair of emerald green eyes gazing down at her.

Todd's eyes are warm brown, she reminded herself. *I'm with him, in Sweet Valley, California, and that's the Pacific Ocean out there,* she thought, shaking her head to clear it.

"Let's take one of those out for a ride," Todd suggested, referring to the canoes stacked upside down on the beach, which were kept on hand for customers of the marina.

Elizabeth shifted uneasily in his arms. "I don't know, Todd. The ocean looks rough tonight."

Todd chuckled softly and ran his hands gently up her arms. "What are you talking about?"

Elizabeth looked at the water and cringed. It was low tide, and the ocean was as calm as she'd ever seen it. "You know how quickly ocean conditions can change," she insisted, groping for excuses.

Todd touched his forehead to hers. "I'm not suggesting that we paddle to Hawaii," he whispered. "Just around the docks."

"But what if we capsize?" she argued.

He touched the side of her face, then rested his arms loosely across her shoulders. "I'm not worried," he assured her. He kissed the bridge of her nose. "You're a strong swimmer. You'll save us."

She shot him a doubtful look. "I don't know. . . ."

"OK, I'll save myself," he quipped.

Elizabeth chewed on her bottom lip and avoided

his gaze. "I'm serious, Todd. What if we get in trouble for taking a canoe?"

"We won't be *taking* a canoe," he countered, "just *borrowing* one for a while."

"But—"

Todd placed his thumb against her lips, interrupting her objections. "Trust me, Elizabeth. It'll be fun," he promised.

Elizabeth exhaled deeply and closed her eyes. Her arguments sounded weak, even to her. When she opened her eyes, Todd was staring at her intently. "OK, sure, let's do it," she agreed reluctantly.

She followed uneasily as Todd sprinted along the dock and back to the beach. "Your pick, Liz," he offered, gesturing with a flourish at the available canoes.

"They all look the same to me," Elizabeth murmured.

Todd laughed. "Yeah, they do, don't they?" He stepped forward and lifted one of the canoes off the stack, letting it topple right-side up next to the pile. "This is going to be great," he declared.

Elizabeth helped him carry the canoe and a set of paddles back to the dock. After Todd hopped into the canoe, he waited for it to stop wobbling, then reached his hand up to help Elizabeth.

But the flood of memories came back, crashing through her mind—a gorgeous face with green eyes that could make her feel hot and cold at the same time. Her mind echoed the name of the guy who'd captured her heart at Camp Echo Mountain—*Joey Mason*. She'd spent so many wonderful hours canoeing with him, sharing their dreams, reveling in being alone together in the deep darkness of Montana nights. Elizabeth could still remember the way it had felt to be in Joey's arms, holding him, kissing him . . .

Elizabeth stepped back, overwhelmed. A small moan escaped her lips. She looked at Todd, and her heart felt as if it were sinking. *I can't get into that canoe,* she realized.

Todd looked at her with concern in his eyes. "What's the matter?" he asked.

Elizabeth pressed her fingers to the side of her head and exhaled. "I have a really bad headache."

"I think a nice, peaceful canoe ride can cure a headache," he said, grinning.

She shook her head. "I should go home."

"But why—"

"Please, Todd," she pleaded, "just take me home. Right now."

Todd threw up his hands, obviously disappointed. "Whatever you say, Elizabeth," he grumbled.

Jessica crawled under the table at which she and her friends had been sitting. She ran her hands along the bottom of the wooden booth in the hope that her earring had rolled into the corner. "It has to be here somewhere."

From underneath a nearby table, Lila groaned. "I just touched a wad of chewed bubble gum."

"Maybe it rolled under a table in the next row," Jessica suggested as she crawled out backward. Bracing herself with one hand on the edge of the table, she rose to her feet and slipped into the booth.

"They've already mopped that section," Lila replied as she stood up and brushed the dust off her tailored linen skirt and silk blouse. "I'll be sending you the dry cleaning bill for this," she said as she plopped down in the seat across from Jessica.

Ignoring Lila's whiny complaints, Jessica snapped her fingers. "The trays! We must have tossed out the earring when we emptied the trays." She jumped out of the booth and ran to the garbage receptacle near the door.

It had already been emptied.

"This isn't good," Lila grumbled, peering over Jessica's shoulder. "Now what?"

"We have to find it," Jessica proclaimed. She hurried over to the counter, where two haggard-looking waitresses were cleaning up and refilling the soft-drink dispensers. "What have you done with the garbage?" Jessica asked in an urgent voice.

The guy who was still mopping the dining room answered. "It's already been dumped," he said.

One of the waitress was scraping a glob of dried ketchup off the counter with a knife. She looked up at Jessica and shrugged. "There's your answer, hon."

"But where?" Jessica demanded.

"The garbage gets dumped out back, behind the building," she replied.

"I need that garbage!" Jessica cried. "My diamond earring might be in it."

The waitress tossed the knife into a plastic bin and untied her apron. "If you girls want to dig through the Dumpster for your diamond, that's your business. We're going home. It's been a long day," she added, brushing back her sweaty dark bangs.

Jessica turned to Lila with a sad-puppy look in her eyes. Lila raised her hands and shook her head. "No way, Jessica. This blouse is a Pierre Jové original."

"Please, Lila, I'm desperate. I can't go home unless I find that earring."

Lila crossed her arms and stared straight ahead. "No. Never. Not on your life."

"But I need your help," Jessica pleaded. Lila squeezed her eyes shut, which Jessica took as a good sign. "That earring means so much to me, Li."

Lila groaned. "Stop it, Jessica!"

"*Please!*" Jessica wailed. "I'll be grateful for the rest of my life, and I promise that if you ever need a really big favor . . ."

Lila fiddled with a straw that had been lying on the counter. "I'd help you, really I would," she insisted. "But it's a lost cause, Jess. You'll never find a tiny earring in a garbage heap."

Jessica blinked hard, squeezing out a few well-timed tears. "We have to try," she wheedled, sniffling. She covered her face with her hands and sobbed dramatically, separating her fingers enough to peek at Lila's expression. *She's cracking,* Jessica thought, relieved.

"I can't believe I'm even considering this," Lila muttered.

Jessica dropped her hands and smiled brightly. "You're the best friend in the whole world," she declared.

Lila put her hands on her hips and flashed Jessica a crooked smile. "You're going to owe me big for this one, Wakefield."

They found a flashlight in the glove compartment of Lila's car and walked around to the back of the building. The Dairi Burger employees were just leaving; one of the waitresses honked as she drove away.

Jessica scowled at the retreating car, then

climbed onto the lid of the Dumpster. "Grab my hand," she instructed, reaching down to help Lila. The loud, banging sounds of their efforts reverberated through the deserted parking lot.

"I have a bad feeling about this, Jess," Lila groaned as she peered into the shadowy interior of the Dumpster. "It stinks too."

Jessica raised her eyebrows. "It's garbage. How do you expect it to smell?"

"There's *so much* of it," Lila whined.

"Let's just get this over with," Jessica said as she tore open one of the black plastic bags. Lila leaned over and helped Jessica pick through the contents.

"Oh, yuck," Lila cried. "I just touched someone's half-eaten burger. This is so *awful*. And there are, like, a million bags in here."

"But the bag we emptied our trays into was the last one they threw out," Jessica reminded her. "So it's probably one of these right on top of the pile."

"Brilliant, Jess. Oh, no! Some jerk threw away a paper cup with a milkshake in it, and everything's all sticky. What a pig!"

"Try not to get emotionally involved," Jessica quipped as she pushed aside a partially eaten fish patty. "Didn't Sandy have the fish fillet special?" she mumbled under her breath, trying to remember. "Hey, Lila, did Sandy eat her whole sandwich?"

"How should I know?" Lila snapped. "Ugh, I think I'm going to puke. This smells so bad. What is this—pantyhose? Oh, yuck! And they're all gooey from the chocolate shake slime. This is hopeless, Jess, not to mention utterly gross. I love diamonds as much as anyone, but I'm not sure if it's worth all this."

"I'm positive this is our garbage bag," Jessica said optimistically. "Look, there's my cheeseburger wrapper."

"There are millions of cheeseburger wrappers in here," Lila pointed out, waving her flashlight over the mess.

Jessica refused to give up hope. "I know my earring is here somewhere. We have to keep looking."

Lila raised her head and frowned. "Did you hear that?"

"What?" Jessica asked. Lila raised her finger to her lips, gesturing for silence. Then Jessica heard it too--the high-pitched howling of a cat.

"Where is it?" Lila whispered as she swept the area with the beam of her flashlight.

Jessica saw a pair of cat eyes flash in a tree at the edge of the lot. "There," she said, abandoning the garbage bag. "Look, it's a white cat. Come on, I think it's stuck."

Lila sniffed. "If you think I'm going to climb a tree in my Pierre Jové, you're crazy."

Jessica lowered herself down the side of the Dumpster. "I'll climb the tree," she said, beckoning to Lila. "But I need you to give me a boost."

Lila glared at her for a few moments, as if trying to think of a reasonable argument. Finally she climbed off the Dumpster, grabbing Jessica's shoulders on the way down to steady herself. She brushed off her outfit and looked up with one eyebrow raised. "Jess, the next time we go out for a Saturday night with the girls, remind me to borrow one of *your* outfits."

Jessica giggled. "Better yet, we'll both borrow something from Elizabeth. Her clothes are perfect for rummaging around in the garbage—everything she owns is machine washable."

Jessica stood at the base of the tree, trying to figure out the best strategy for reaching the cat, which was still meowing desperately. "This place is so eerie without any people," Lila whispered. "And that cat is giving me the creeps."

"Relax," Jessica said. "The poor little thing is probably just scared and lonely."

"I am too," Lila murmured. "Let's hurry."

As Lila boosted her up to the first branch, Jessica remembered the last time she'd climbed a tree. It had been with Paul at Camp Echo Mountain. She smiled at the memory as she pulled herself up to the next branch.

23

When she'd finally reached the branch where the cat was perched, Jessica paused for a moment. "You're just a kitten," she murmured. "And you're so pretty." The kitten was white with gray markings on its head and back. It watched warily, then hissed as Jessica inched her way closer.

When she was a few feet away from the kitten, Jessica held out her hand. "It's OK," she said softly, coaxing it to come to her. She scooped up the kitten in her arms and waited for it to calm down a bit.

Jessica climbed down the tree with the kitten in her hand and held it out to Lila. "See?" Jessica remarked. "She isn't creepy at all. She's adorable." Jessica hugged the bundle of fur in her arms and looked into its eyes. "Guess what, Lila. I just found a new Wakefield pet," she declared.

Lila snorted. "I'm sure your dog will be thrilled."

In the dark shadows behind the Dairi Burger, a guy stood motionless as he watched the two girls in the moonlit parking lot. They were both lovely, but it was the one with long blond hair who captured his attention, mesmerizing him with her beauty.

Everything about her pulsed with life—her graceful, athletic movements when she'd climbed the tree to rescue the animal, her musical laughter,

24

the light in her eyes. She was so perfect, she made his heart beat painfully.

He imagined holding her in his arms, his lips moving across her face, down her long, slender neck. *Her skin would be soft and taste so sweet,* he thought.

Pulling himself away from his fantasy, he silently crouched down and wiped his bloody hands on the grass. Then, with one last longing look at the girls, he disappeared into the night.

"You're such a pretty little thing," Jessica cooed as she nuzzled the kitten's soft white and gray fur. "OK, Lila, back to the garbage heap."

"I was hoping you'd forgotten about the earring," Lila grumbled.

Still holding her new kitten, Jessica pulled herself up to the top of the Dumpster with one hand. "Let's be organized about this," she suggested. "I'll pull the bags out and you spread the stuff out on the ground."

Lila muttered something incoherent, which Jessica took to mean yes. She lowered herself into the Dumpster and pulled out another garbage bag. In her hand, the kitten began to hiss. "Hush," Jessica said, stroking its soft fur. "This place doesn't smell any worse than gourmet cat food, so quit complaining."

"Oh, gross—this bag is full of paper towels and tissues," Lila whined. "It probably came from the rest rooms." Suddenly she screamed.

"What's the matter?" Jessica asked.

"I just stepped on a dirty diaper!" Lila wailed. "This is so *horrible*."

Jessica's foot hit something solid at the bottom of the Dumpster. Curious, she began pulling off the bags on top of it to get a better look.

"Quit throwing those out so fast," Lila complained. "You're getting them mixed up with the junk I've already picked through."

"There's something under here," Jessica said. "Give me the flashlight."

"Unless it's your diamond earring, it doesn't matter," Lila replied as she handed the flashlight up to Jessica. "We're not here to explore."

"Hold on, I've almost got it." Jessica pushed aside the last few bags and shone the light on the floor of the Dumpster—illuminating the ghostly white face of a dead body.

Jessica screamed and instantly hoisted herself out of the Dumpster. Lila grabbed the flashlight from Jessica and peered inside—and screamed too.

Squeezing the kitten to her chest, Jessica forced herself to take another look. The body was that of a young man, dressed in jeans and a blue sweater. "What's that mark on his neck?" she whispered. "Lila, shine the flashlight on that dark spot on his neck."

Lila shook her head frantically, still screaming. Jessica took the flashlight from her and pointed the beam at the guy's neck, where she saw something resembling teeth marks. She stepped back, horrified. "It looks like he's been *bitten!*" Jessica exclaimed. "By a wild animal!"

Chapter 3

Jessica and Lila clung to each other, both of them shaking, holding the kitten between them. They'd phoned the police from Lila's car phone, and within minutes the lot behind the Dairi Burger had sprung to life with screaming sirens and flashing lights. Surrounded by the frenzy, the kitten seemed hysterical. It screeched and howled as if it were in pain and clawed at Jessica's denim jacket.

A few yards away, a police officer leaned against a cruiser, speaking into the radio, describing the victim. "Caucasian, male . . . late teens to early twenties . . . five feet, eleven inches, estimated one-ninety pounds . . . apparent cause of death—" The officer paused in midsentence. Jessica watched as he pulled out a white handkerchief and wiped it across his forehead. His hand shook slightly. "Unidentified animal bite to the neck," he continued. "It looks as if—" Again he paused. "As if the blood has been drained from the victim's body."

Jessica closed her eyes. *This can't really be happening,* she thought. The horror seemed unreal. She felt as if she might wake up any minute to find herself in bed in her own room at home across town on Calico Drive.

A tall man with short red hair rushed over to them, clutching a notebook. "Eric Garnet, *Sweet Valley News.* I understand you girls discovered the body while you were searching for a diamond earring."

Jessica sniffed. "I was the one who actually found the body." From behind the reporter, a bright light flashed in Jessica's eyes, startling her.

"Sorry about that," Mr. Garnet said as he introduced the *Sweet Valley News* photographer.

Jessica licked her lips and pushed back her hair. "That's quite all right," she replied, automatically striking a pose for the camera as she blinked away the red dots before her eyes. "News is news. People have to know what happened here tonight."

"I'm glad you understand," Mr. Garnet said. "Is the earring you're wearing the match to the one you lost?"

Jessica nodded. "They were a gift from my

grandmother. I feel terrible about losing it. But of course, I feel worse about the poor guy who was murdered." She was pleased to see that Mr. Garnet was writing furiously in his notebook.

"Come on, Eric," the photographer called. "They're taking out the body."

Everyone's attention turned to the Dumpster, where a team of police officers was lifting out a stretcher to which the victim's body had been strapped. Lila squeezed her eyes shut and groaned, but Jessica felt compelled to look. His arms were dangling off the stretcher. There was a gold watch on his wrist.

The kitten howled frantically and dug its claws into Jessica's neck. Jessica yelped in pain and grabbed its front paws. Holding them firmly in her hand, Jessica looked down into the kitten's slanted yellow eyes. "She's as scared as we are," Jessica commented to Lila.

Still squeezing her eyes shut, Lila nodded.

Officer Reyes of the Sweet Valley Police Department walked over to them. "This must have been a frightening experience for you girls."

Lila opened her eyes wide and nodded.

"We'll try to get you out of here as soon as possible," he assured them. "Let's see if we have the facts straight." Reading from a clipboard, he began, "You were searching through the Dumpster for a

31

diamond earring when you discovered the body."

Lila and Jessica nodded.

Another police officer, a woman with red hair, came over to him. "We have a confirmation on the victim's identity," she announced. "Dean Maddingly, age seventeen, from Big Mesa." She shook her head gravely. "He was last seen alive one hour ago."

Jessica closed her eyes and shuddered. *He was only a year older than me,* she realized. *And he was killed while I was sitting inside the Dairi Burger with my friends.*

Officer Reyes wrote something on his clipboard and turned back to Lila and Jessica. "Do you remember hearing or seeing anything strange out here before you discovered the body?" he asked.

"Just this cat," Jessica replied. "She was up the tree, meowing."

"Excuse me, Jessica," Eric Garnet said. "Can we get a photo of you and the cat in front of the Dumpster?"

Jessica shrugged. "Sure. Where do you want me to stand?"

The photographer issued a few directions. "Put your hand under the kitten's chin, and tuck your hair behind your ears so we can see the one earring."

Jessica loved modeling and was more than happy to comply. She pushed the gruesome horror out of her mind and concentrated on presenting a polished image for the camera.

The kitten, however, was not so easily distracted. She hissed and growled. At one point she clawed at Jessica, managing to rip out a few strands of her long blond hair.

Officer Reyes stared at the kitten squirming in Jessica's arms. "I suspect that cat was the only witness to this horrible, brutal murder. If only animals could talk," he said, shaking his head.

The heavy silence in Todd's BMW pressed down on him like a load of bricks. From the corner of his eye, he could see Elizabeth staring straight ahead with a glassy look in her blue-green eyes. She seemed to be a thousand miles away. *What is going on with her?* Todd wondered.

He knew Elizabeth well enough to guess that something serious was on her mind. *But what?* he thought, racking his brains. *Did I do or say something wrong?*

He mentally ran through the events of the evening, trying to find a clue to explain Elizabeth's odd behavior. He'd brought her flowers and a bottle of chilled sparkling cider that he knew she liked. He'd remembered to tell her how nice she looked, how great the picnic stuff was. He'd listened to her ideas about the "Personal Profiles" column she was writing about her friend Maria Slater for the school paper—

"Look out, Todd," Elizabeth warned.

He blinked and automatically hit the brakes. A car had swerved into his lane, nearly colliding with the van in front of him. Todd stopped just short of hitting them both.

"You shouldn't follow so closely," Elizabeth said.

Todd nodded, banking his irritation and the sarcastic comment on the tip of his tongue. *After all we've meant to each other, that's the only thing she has to say to me?* he thought. Obviously she was angry at him about something.

But what? he asked himself. After their picnic dinner on the beach that evening, he and Elizabeth had walked hand in hand along the water. He'd even mentioned how beautiful the crescent moon was. *Flowers, picnic at the beach, moonlight, just the two of us . . .* Todd shook his head, bewildered. As far as he could see, it had been Elizabeth's idea of the perfect date.

Did I talk too much about basketball? He squinted as he thought hard. As far as he could remember, he hadn't even mentioned sports or the SVH basketball team all evening. He'd recently spent a month at basketball camp in Los Angeles, working with professional basketball coaches—and he'd hardly told her anything about it. He also realized that she hadn't asked.

Todd glanced at her again. The unhappy look on her face tore at his heart. Part of him was tempted to pull over and demand an explanation. But the other part of him was afraid of what her explanation might be.

He gripped the steering wheel tightly, his frustration rising. He hated it when Elizabeth put distance between them.

Elizabeth noticed Todd glancing at her with a questioning look in his eyes. She knew her behavior that evening had probably thrown him into a state of confusion. *Join the club, Todd,* she thought. She didn't know what was going on either.

A sharp pain throbbed in her temples. *I guess the headache wasn't a lie after all,* she thought wryly as she rubbed her head with her fingertips.

Elizabeth glanced at Todd as the car passed under the light of a streetlamp, illuminating the sharp, handsome features of his face. She tried to remember how her heart had fluttered the first time he'd kissed her.

They'd had problems in the past, but always their love for each other had brought them back together. *I still love him, don't I?* she wondered. But it was as if Elizabeth's feelings for Todd were wrapped in cotton. And she didn't know what to do about it or what would happen to their relationship.

Todd turned onto Calico Drive, and Elizabeth sighed, relieved that the torturous ride was nearly over. But all thoughts of her and Todd vanished as the Wakefield home came into sight and Elizabeth saw the police car parked out front.

A million horrible possibilities ran through her mind—*Jessica hurt . . . our parents . . . a car accident . . . a burglary . . .* Her heart felt as if it were stuck in her throat.

Todd pulled into the driveway and came to a screeching stop. Elizabeth jumped out of the car and ran into the house, with Todd following close behind. Her panic level shot higher when she found a uniformed police officer in the living room, talking with her parents and Jessica.

"What's going on?" Elizabeth demanded.

Jessica ran over to her and hugged her tightly. "I'm so glad you're home, Liz," she cried.

Something sharp poked into Elizabeth's arm. She yelped in pain and stepped back, just noticing the kitten squirming in Jessica's arms.

"This is Jasmine, our new pet," Jessica told her in a shaky voice. "I've already introduced her to Prince Albert, but he wasn't very impressed," she said, referring to the Wakefields' golden Labrador.

Elizabeth rubbed the claw mark on her arm and turned to her parents, who were sitting side by side on the couch, grave expressions on their faces. Alice Wakefield usually shared the same fair, peach-toned complexion as her daughters. But that night Elizabeth's mother's face was stark white with obvious fear.

"What's going on?" Elizabeth asked again.

"This is Officer Reyes," her father said. "There was a murder in Sweet Valley. Jessica and Lila discovered the victim's body behind the Dairi Burger."

Elizabeth gasped. Standing next to her, Todd blanched. "It was terrible," Jessica said, shaking her head. Even the kitten seemed unsettled, squirming under Jessica's neck as if trying to find a place to hide.

"Who?" Todd asked in a thin voice.

"The victim was from Big Mesa," Officer Reyes answered. "Dean Maddingly."

Todd nodded. "I've heard the name. He's a track runner, isn't he?"

"We don't have a complete profile as of yet," the officer told them. "His body was found in the Dumpster in the Dairi Burger's back parking lot."

Elizabeth turned to her sister, nonplussed. "What were you and Lila doing in the Dumpster?"

"I lost one of my new diamond earrings, and I

37

thought it might have been thrown out by mistake," Jessica explained. "The workers at the Dairi Burger had already dumped the trash, and Lila and I were combing through the Dumpster when—" Jessica sucked in a deep, shaky breath and shuddered visibly.

"Are you sure it was murder?" Todd asked the officer.

Jessica flashed Todd an irritated look. "Of course it was. Guys don't usually climb into Dumpsters to take a nap and then pass away in their sleep."

Elizabeth glared at her sister, then directed the same question to the police officer. He nodded gravely. "The victim died from loss of blood," he said. "It had been drained from the body and removed from the scene."

A fist of cold dread gripped Elizabeth's heart as she listened to the details of the murder. *Something is wrong in Sweet Valley*, she thought. *And it isn't going to end with this murder.* Experience had taught her to listen to her gut feelings; more often than not, they were right.

"You mean someone *stole* the guy's blood?" Todd asked.

Jessica seemed about to say something sarcastic, but Elizabeth silenced her with a stern look and asked her about the cat.

"Lila and I found Jasmine freaking out in a tree near the Dumpster," Jessica said, holding the kitten up for Elizabeth's inspection. "She's pretty upset still, but I'm hoping she'll calm down with a bit of tender loving care."

Elizabeth took the animal from Jessica, avoiding its flailing claws, and stroked the kitten's soft fur.

"We think she may have witnessed the murder," Jessica said.

Elizabeth stared into the kitten's narrow yellow eyes and wondered what they had seen that night. *What story would you tell?* she thought.

Chapter 4

"I can't imagine this story *not* being picked up by the national news," Jessica said on the way to school Monday morning. "Maybe even a true-crime show. But I'm going to insist that they let me play myself in the dramatic reenactment. I'm not about to hand over my role to a professional actress. After all, no one else could possibly understand the emotions I felt that night."

Elizabeth was driving the Jeep, dreading each mile that brought them closer to Sweet Valley High. Unlike her twin, she hadn't recovered from the weekend. If anything, her feeling of foreboding had only grown worse. Between Joey's letter, her date with Todd, and the murder, Elizabeth felt as if her stomach had been invaded by bumblebees.

"What do you think?" Jessica asked.

Elizabeth glanced sideways at her twin. "About what?"

Jessica exhaled loudly, clearly exasperated. "Playing ourselves in the dramatic reenactment. I suppose I could play your part if you're not interested."

Elizabeth slowed the Jeep as they approached the line of cars waiting to turn into the school driveway. "Jessica, a guy was murdered. How can you possibly be thinking of your acting career?"

"It's horrible that he died, I agree," Jessica replied. "But isn't it best to look on the bright side? You know, search for the silver lining, the glass half full and all that? Maybe we can have a dedication to him in the credits after the show."

Elizabeth rolled her eyes. "You're something else."

Jessica giggled. "Thanks. Even though I'm sure you didn't mean it as a compliment."

"I don't understand how you can be in such a good mood," Elizabeth said. "A deranged killer is still out there somewhere. And I'm sure everyone read the story in the paper yesterday—the whole school is going to be talking about the murder."

Jessica smiled brightly. "I know. But I've never been one to shy away from the limelight."

Elizabeth's sarcastic retort died on her lips as she spotted Todd's black BMW a few cars ahead of the Jeep. She quickly averted her gaze. *I hope he doesn't notice me,* she thought, keeping her eyes focused on the traffic guard as though the gray-haired woman were the most interesting sight in the world.

When Elizabeth drove into the school lot, she parked far away from Todd's car, hoping to avoid him for a while longer. She knew she owed him an explanation after her behavior at the marina Saturday night, but she didn't have the energy to face him just then.

Jessica scowled at her. "Why are you parking over here? There are plenty of empty spaces closer to the entrance."

Elizabeth turned off the engine and pocketed the keys. "I need the exercise."

Jessica jumped out, grumbling, and stormed off in a huff. Elizabeth followed at a much slower pace, trying to calm her growing anxiety.

The school hallways were as chaotic as usual that morning, packed with students moving at various speeds, shouting greetings, slamming lockers, and pushing their way through the crowd. As Elizabeth made her way toward her locker, she felt herself being shoved from behind. "Hey, watch where you're going!" she protested.

As if he hadn't heard her, a tall, lanky guy wearing black leather pants pushed her out of his way and continued walking down the hall. Fuming, Elizabeth glared at his retreating back.

A short distance away, Peggy Abbot was balancing a pile of books and a papier-mâché creation on her knee as she attempted to open the door to Mr. Jaworski's classroom. The guy in black bumped into her, pushing her into the wall and knocking everything out of her hands. Without a backward glance, he kept going, as if people were nothing more than minor obstacles in his path. *Who does he think he is?* Elizabeth thought hotly.

"Are you OK, Peggy?" she asked as she bent down to help pick up the fallen books.

"Oh, sure," Peggy said, pushing back her dark hair. "But my history project isn't feeling so great."

Elizabeth looked at the crumpled mess of papier-mâché on the floor and clenched her fists angrily. "That jerk stepped on it!" Although Peggy Abbot wasn't one of her favorite people, Elizabeth felt terrible for her.

Peggy shrugged. "It was supposed to be an English castle."

"Do you know who that guy is?" Elizabeth asked, primed for battle.

Peggy shook her head. "He was hot, though, don't you think?"

Elizabeth glared at her in disbelief. "How can you say that? He ruined your project."

The other girl laughed loudly. Jessica had once remarked that Peggy sounded like a donkey when she laughed, and Elizabeth had to agree.

"How can you think about schoolwork when a gorgeous hunk like that walks by?" Peggy asked. "I know Todd is great and all, but that guy—" She fanned herself with a notebook and whistled.

Elizabeth wrinkled her nose and handed over Peggy's books. "See you later," she said, anxious to get away from the silly girl.

"Then we heard a cat meowing in a tree near the edge of the lot," Jessica told the crowd gathered around her and Lila at their lockers that morning.

"Actually, the cat was *howling*," Lila clarified. "We think it might have witnessed the murder, because it was acting so crazy. It kept clawing and hissing. Jessica's neck was bleeding from all the scratches."

Responding to the cue, Jessica pushed her hair back and tipped her head, giving the audience a better view. "When I saw my neck in the mirror Sunday morning, I was so shocked. It looked as if I'd been wrestling a mountain lion."

"Ouch," Annie murmured. "That looks like it must've hurt."

"It did," Jessica replied. "But I couldn't just

leave the poor kitten in the deserted parking lot. Especially when she'd been so traumatized."

"Too bad the cat can't talk," Amy said pensively.

Winston Egbert's eyes widened. "A computer!" he interjected. "I saw a movie once where they plugged a computer into a giraffe's brain and—"

Jessica raised her eyebrows and stared at him wryly. "I'm sure it was the highlight of your life," she drawled. Everyone laughed, including Winston. Maria Santelli hugged his arm and kissed the side of his face.

Jessica shook her head. She couldn't figure out what Maria, a popular girl and a cheerleader, saw in Winston. He was a class-clown nerd with a twisted sense of humor. Although Elizabeth considered him to be one of her closest friends, Jessica had much higher standards for friends, and extra-high standards for boyfriends.

"Was that the cat you were holding in the photo in yesterday's paper?" Sandy asked.

Jessica smiled, beaming. "Wasn't that a cute picture of us? It's easy to see why we made the front page of the Sunday edition."

Lila snorted. "Sure, Jessica. Every murder report should be accompanied by a *cute* photograph."

Jessica shoved her playfully. "You're just jealous because you weren't on the front page."

"No, I'm not," Lila countered. "Believe it or not, everyone in the world doesn't automatically think photo opportunity when they stumble on a dead body."

"That's right," Jessica said. "You were worried about soiling your precious Pierre Jové silk blouse."

Sandy shivered, gazing at them with a look of concern. "I still can't believe all that happened at the Dairi Burger—right after we left."

Aaron Dallas let out a small laugh. "You sure have a way of finding trouble, Jessica."

Amy giggled. "I guess we took off just in time," she said. "Were your parents mad when they found out you'd lost your diamond earring?"

"They were too upset about a murderer being loose in Sweet Valley to worry about jewelry. And I still have this one," Jessica remarked, turning her head to show off the remaining earring in her left ear.

Bruce Patman shook his head, laughing. "With the story of your missing earring on the front page of the Sunday paper, I'd love to see what's happening at the town dump this morning. I'll bet it's crawling with derelicts trying to find the Jessica Wakefield diamond."

Just then, Principal "Chrome Dome" Cooper's voice came over the PA system, announcing that there would be an emergency assembly first period.

"How convenient," Jessica said as she slammed her locker door shut. "I was wondering if I'd get a chance to do my history homework before class this morning."

Elizabeth and her best friend, Enid Rollins, joined the throng of students filing into the auditorium for the assembly. "What else did the police say?" Enid asked. "Do they have any clues?"

"Just what I told you," Elizabeth murmured.

"So why didn't you call me back yesterday?" Enid asked, an accusing tone creeping into her voice. "I was so shocked when I read the paper yesterday, and I nearly went crazy wondering what was going on. I stayed in the house all day so I wouldn't miss your call."

"I'm sorry," Elizabeth said, wishing Enid would drop the subject. "I slept most of the day. I was exhausted from staying up all night with Jessica on Saturday."

Enid turned to her with a sympathetic look. "It must have been horrible," Enid remarked. "Imagine finding a dead body instead of an earring. Did the police say if there had been other murders like this one recently? Do they know what kind of animal bite it was they found on the body?"

"There's Maria," Elizabeth said, waving to a girl seated near the front of the auditorium—and leaving Enid's questions unanswered. Maria Slater was a childhood friend of Elizabeth's who had recently moved back to Sweet Valley.

Although Maria had "retired" from her successful career as a child actress when she was twelve, she still looked every bit the star. She'd grown taller since middle school and wore her hair much shorter, which gave her an elegant, sophisticated look. Her ebony complexion was flawless, and her dark eyes were large and set wide apart. But despite her fashion-model beauty, Maria wasn't interested in rekindling her acting career. She was more interested in writing and literature, as Elizabeth was.

She and Maria had renewed their friendship at Camp Echo Mountain in Montana, where they'd both spent a month working as junior counselors. It was at Camp Echo Mountain that Elizabeth had met and fallen hard for Joey.

Maria gestured enthusiastically for them to join her.

"Come on, Enid, let's go sit up there with Maria," Elizabeth suggested.

"I don't know," Enid grumbled. "She's sitting awfully close to the stage."

Elizabeth frowned. "So? This isn't a movie theater."

"There are plenty of seats on this side. Why don't we just sit here?" Enid said.

"Because Maria saved seats for us," Elizabeth insisted firmly.

Enid threw up her hands and exhaled loudly. "Fine. Let's go sit with Maria."

As they made their way across the auditorium, Elizabeth puzzled over Enid's grumpy attitude that morning. *I'll have to ask her about it later,* she thought.

"Hi, guys," Maria greeted them cheerfully.

Elizabeth sat down next to her. Enid took the seat on the other side of Elizabeth.

"Seems you've had an exciting weekend," Maria said pointedly. "Or at least Jessica did. Do you know if the police have any suspects?"

Elizabeth shook her head weakly. "I really don't want to talk about it."

"But Liz, we should know if there's a deranged serial killer out there," Enid protested.

"Sorry," Elizabeth muttered. She turned to Maria with a meaningful look. "I have something to show you." Elizabeth fumbled through her backpack and pulled out the letter that had twisted her heart into knots. "Three guesses who it's from," she challenged as she handed it to Maria.

Maria raised her eyebrows and silently mouthed, "Joey?" Elizabeth nodded solemnly.

"Who is it from?" Enid asked.

"A guy I met at camp," Elizabeth answered over

her shoulder. She had avoided telling Enid about Joey because it would have made him—and their relationship—seem too real. *But he is real, and you did have a romance with him,* Elizabeth objected inwardly. "What should I do?" she asked Maria.

Maria's scanned the letter and looked up with an alarmed expression in her eyes. "Oh, my gosh, he's transferring to UCLA! He's going to be living within driving distance. This could seriously effect your life, Liz."

Enid leaned closer. "How will w*hat* effect your life?"

"I'm still not sure if I want to see him again," Elizabeth told Maria. "No, that's not really true. I'm not sure if I *should* see him. But I do want to."

Maria nodded, catching her bottom lip between her teeth. "You'd better think this one through very carefully. Joey is terrific, I know, but you and Todd—"

"Elizabeth, will you *please* tell me what's going on?" Enid demanded.

Elizabeth sighed wearily. She felt terribly confused about Joey and couldn't bear to rehash the gory details of her dilemma, especially in a crowded auditorium. "I can't go into it right now," she told Enid. "Maybe later, OK?"

"Fine," Enid replied tersely.

Mr. Cooper stepped up to the podium on the stage and quieted the students. "Good morning. May I have your attention, please?" The bright stage lights cast a shiny reflection on his bald head.

Sitting in the back row of the auditorium, Jessica balanced her history textbook and notebook on her lap as she frantically scribbled her essay about the impact of World War I on the women's suffrage movement.

"We have received some distressing news regarding an incident that took place in Sweet Valley over the weekend," Mr. Cooper announced.

Jessica half listened as the principal gave a brief account of the murder that had happened on Saturday night. She caught a few curious glances from some of the people sitting near her. *I guess it is my story,* she reminded herself as she acknowledged their attention with a brief smile.

"The Sweet Valley police are making every conceivable effort to apprehend the killer," Mr. Cooper assured them. "In the meantime, however, it's very important that everyone exercise extreme caution. We are advising students to practice common sense—to avoid desolate areas, especially at night, and to report any suspicious activity to the police. We still don't know what we're dealing with, I'm afraid."

No kidding, Chrome Dome, Jessica thought as she lowered her head and returned to her history assignment. *Let's see . . .* "After World War I, the *Nineteenth Amendment gave women the right to vote, in 1920 . . .*"

Jessica stopped reading and wrinkled her nose in distaste. She couldn't understand why Elizabeth found history so fascinating. *History is either utterly boring or terribly depressing—or both,* she thought.

On the stage, Mr. Cooper cleared his throat loudly. "And now I'd like to share with you some lighter news."

Jessica pushed her hair behind her ear with the cap of her pen and looked up, curious to hear Chrome Dome's announcement.

"I'd like to introduce Jonathan Cain, a senior transfer student to Sweet Valley High." Mr. Cooper motioned to someone in the first row. "Please stand up and take a bow, Jonathan."

A tall, lanky guy wearing black leather pants and a black T-shirt stood up and turned to the group. Jessica inhaled sharply, her eyes wide as she studied the gorgeous new student. *Just when I thought there wasn't anyone interesting at Sweet Valley High!* she thought excitedly.

He turned to sit back down, but Mr. Cooper flicked his hand, gesturing for him to remain standing. Jessica's pulse quickened and her mouth

53

went dry as Jonathan Cain turned around again slowly. A lock of jet black hair fell across his forehead. He absently pushed it back with the back of his hand; the small movement seemed incredibly sexy. *He's totally hot!* she thought.

His eyes were fascinatingly beautiful. Jessica regretted sitting so far back that she couldn't see what color they were. His eyebrows were thick and as dark as his hair, making his skin seem very pale in contrast. He had sexy deep red lips, which Jessica noticed were turned up slightly at the corners, as if he found all the attention amusing.

"Jonathan has been living abroad," Mr. Cooper explained. "He has attended schools in Sweden, Greece, and most recently England. . . ."

Jessica was completely mesmerized. Her palms were sweaty, and she could hardly catch her breath. He was the most gorgeous guy she'd ever seen. *He will be mine,* she vowed. *Soon.*

Enid sat glumly in the auditorium, feeling like a total third wheel. Next to her, Elizabeth and Maria were scribbling messages back and forth in an open notebook. For some time now, Elizabeth hadn't been acting like Enid's best friend. *She's been acting like* Maria's *best friend,* Enid thought hotly.

Out of the corner of her eye, she saw Elizabeth

drop the notebook. Maria laughed softly as she and Elizabeth groped under their seats for it.

Enid felt her throat tighten as she watched them. Elizabeth used to talk to her about everything, but now it was Maria she turned to—and that hurt Enid deeply.

Maria retrieved the notebook and passed it back to Elizabeth. Enid sniffed and folded her arms. Forcing herself to ignore them, she faced forward—and her heart stopped. Standing in the front row was the most beautiful man she'd ever seen. All her thoughts of Maria and Elizabeth were completely forgotten as she listened to what Mr. Cooper was saying.

". . . and I know you'll all join me in welcoming Jonathan Cain to Sweet Valley High and in wishing him the utmost success."

Jonathan Cain, Enid repeated silently. *Even his name sounds beautiful.* She stared into his deep blue eyes and felt utterly captivated by their intensity. *I've just met my soul mate,* she decided with complete certainty.

That's him! Elizabeth realized. *Jonathan Cain.* The creep who had nearly knocked her down that morning was standing up in the front row, smirking at the audience. And Mr. Cooper was going on about him as if the jerk were the new crowned prince of Sweet Valley. *What is going on?* she wondered.

Jonathan turned his head slightly and looked right at her with blue eyes that seemed ice cold and feverishly hot at the same time. Elizabeth shuddered as a wave of nausea passed over her. She had a bad feeling about Jonathan Cain.

Chapter 5

"I think I'll get myself a pair of black leather pants," Winston told Todd as they made their way through the food line at lunchtime. "Did you see the girls ogling that new guy in assembly this morning?"

Barely listening to his friend's lighthearted chatter, Todd grunted in reply. His mind was still whirling from the puzzle of Elizabeth's strange behavior during their date on Saturday night. He'd been thinking of her nonstop for two days, and his brain felt as if it were tied up in knots. His confusion had grown to a state of near panic. He couldn't get the question out of his head: *Why has she been acting so cool toward me lately?*

After he'd purchased his lunch, Todd scanned the crowded cafeteria, looking for Elizabeth. Winston came up behind him and asked, "Where are we sitting?"

Todd spotted his girlfriend at a table with Maria Slater. "Listen, Winston," he said, "I really need to talk to Elizabeth alone."

Winston glanced at him with an understanding look and nodded. Then he added jokingly, "Ask her what she thinks of black leather pants."

Shaking his head at the silly remark, Todd headed toward Elizabeth's table. As he got closer, he stopped and watched her for a few seconds. She was wearing a pink sweater that made her face seem as though it were glowing. The diamond earrings in her ears sparkled like stars.

She was talking to Maria about something serious; Todd recognized the small wrinkle between her eyebrows that always appeared when she was thinking hard or saying something important. *Is she telling Maria that she doesn't love me anymore?* he wondered. His heart squeezed painfully at the thought of losing her.

As he approached their table, Elizabeth and Maria's conversation instantly stopped. Elizabeth turned to him with a startled look in her blue-green eyes. *Sure looks like it,* Todd thought. *They were talking about me.*

He swallowed hard and plunked his tray down on the table. He no longer wondered if something was terribly wrong—because now, in his gut, he was certain.

He sat down across from Elizabeth and took a deep, steadying breath. "Liz, can I talk to you privately?" he asked. He glanced at Maria with a pleading look.

Maria gave him a tight smile and discreetly picked up her tray. "See you later, guys."

The tension at the table seemed to grow after Maria had gone. Now that Todd finally had Elizabeth alone, he wasn't sure where to begin. Part of him wanted to know what was going on, but another part of him was afraid that the truth was going to hurt badly.

But he couldn't go on as he had been, scared and anxious and not knowing what was about to happen—or why. Gripping the edges of his tray, Todd took another deep breath and braced himself. "What's going on, Liz?"

She looked at him with a tortured expression in her eyes that tore at his heart. "Maria and I were just going over some details about the *Oracle*. I'm writing about her in 'Personality Profiles' for the next issue. I told you about it last week, remember?"

Todd shook his head. "That's not what I mean. I'm talking about the way you've been acting lately. I know you're keeping something from me."

She blinked. A bright pink flush rose in her cheeks. "I don't understand what—"

"I think you do," Todd interrupted softly.

"No, I don't," she insisted, twisting a napkin in her hands. "I'm not keeping anything from you, I swear."

They're the right words, Todd thought, *but she doesn't mean them.* He noticed that Elizabeth wasn't looking him in the eye.

He poked a straw into his milk carton and unwrapped his sandwich, stalling for time. *Should I just come out and call her a liar?* he wondered.

Before he had a chance to say anything more, Elizabeth gasped. "Oh, no!" she exclaimed, glancing at her watch. "I just remembered I have to print something out in the *Oracle* office before my next class." With that, she grabbed her things and rushed off as if she were being chased by a pack of dogs.

Todd watched her go, feeling more frustrated than ever. He clenched his fists, crushing the milk carton in his hand. A spray of milk spewed out, and he jumped, cursing, as milk splashed all over him, the table, and the floor. *It can't get any worse than this,* he told himself.

Jessica studied her reflection in the mirror above the sinks in the girls' room. *I can't believe this day is almost over,* she thought.

Standing next to her, Lila gushed on and on about Bo—as usual. Jessica did her best to ignore her. She had more important things on her mind, after all. Last period was about to start any minute, and she still hadn't gotten a chance to meet Jonathan Cain.

She'd looked for him between every class and during lunch. She'd even gone to the office during her free period with a flimsy question about the upcoming college fair, hoping that Jonathan's schedule would be lying on the secretary's desk. Unfortunately, Rosemary, Chrome Dome's secretary, had mistaken Jessica's question for genuine interest and proceeded to waste the entire period demonstrating the school's new computerized college-data system.

This is my final chance, Jessica realized as she dabbed some of Lila's perfume behind her ears. It was time to step up the search.

"Go easy with that stuff," Lila protested. "That's real French perfume; you don't have to bathe in it."

Jessica sniffed. "I do smell like I've been hit with a flower truck. If I had known that a sexy, wonderful guy was going to land in Sweet Valley High today, I would have brought my bottle of Rendezvous. It's still my favorite."

"Yours?" Lila asked pointedly.

Jessica giggled. "OK, *Elizabeth's* Rendezvous." She handed the small crystal bottle of perfume back to Lila and pulled out a tube of lipstick.

Lila gathered her things and shoved them into her bag. "You'd better hurry, Jess. The bell's going to ring in a few seconds."

Jessica pulled open her mascara wand. "You go ahead. I'm skipping my last class."

"But you have French this period," Lila said, sounding incredulous.

"So what?" Jessica added a few more strokes of mascara to her left eye and leaned back, studying the result before moving on to the right eye.

"French is one of the few classes offered at SVH that's worth attending," Lila declared. "Bo says that French novels are the most lushly romantic in the world, but unless you read them in the original language, you miss most of the subtle richness of the text."

Jessica paused, holding the mascara wand in midair, and glared at Lila in the mirror. "Lushly romantic? Subtle richness? He really talks like that?"

"Oh, yes," Lila replied, her eyes flashing excitedly. "He is *so* sophisticated. His mother is French, you know. And he's also fluent in Italian and German."

Jessica brushed on a few more strokes of mascara, then began gathering her makeup, brushes, and combs, which were strewn across three sinks. "I would love to hear more on this fascinating topic," she drawled sarcastically, "but really, I have to go."

"Go where?" Lila asked.

Jessica smiled. "I'll tell you all about it later," she said with a jaunty little wave.

The bell had just stopped ringing as Jessica brazenly walked out the side door to the student parking lot. Swinging her arms, she headed to the twins' Jeep and started the engine.

I'll know you when I see you, Jessica thought as she cruised the lot, trying to figure out which vehicle belonged to Jonathan Cain. *I'm sure it's something impressive, unique, and . . . dangerous,* she guessed.

When Jessica saw a huge Harley parked near the edge of the lot, she grinned. "Jonathan would drive something just like that," she whispered to herself.

She parked the Jeep next to the motorcycle and rolled down the window. It was a handsome bike, black with silver stripes. She imagined riding on it through Sweet Valley, with her arms wrapped around Jonathan's lean waist, taking the winding road up to Miller's Point at a dizzying speed. *We're going to have a good time,* she decided.

She checked her appearance once more in the

rearview mirror, then pulled out the latest issue of *Ingenue*, her favorite fashion magazine, to browse through as she waited.

She gave a silent cheer when the shrill sound of the dismissal bell rang out from the building. A few seconds later, students began streaming out the front doors. Jessica scanned the crowd for the gorgeous face she'd been searching for all day. A few minutes later she spotted him. With a sharp intake of breath and a quickening in her heart, she noticed that he was heading in her direction. *I knew it was his bike,* she thought excitedly.

She felt dizzy just watching him walk. He moved with the sleek, powerful grace of a tiger—dangerous, enticing, and terribly sexy. *He's incredible,* she thought.

As he came closer Jessica tore her gaze away and pretended to be engrossed in her magazine. *I don't want to look too anxious,* she reasoned. She was sure that Jonathan would notice her and make the first move. *A guy that hot won't pass up the opportunity to meet someone like me.* But there was nothing wrong with making it a little easier for him.

She caught a glimpse of him over the top of the magazine as he walked by the Jeep to his motorcycle. Her heart began to thump wildly as his shadow fell across the magazine page. *He's prob-*

ably watching me! she thought triumphantly. She waited for him to say something. When he didn't, she chuckled softly, figuring he was shy.

Putting on her sexiest, most welcoming smile, Jessica turned to face him through the open window. "Hi—"

The rest of her greeting was cut off by the roar of the motorcycle's engine. To her surprise, Jonathan peeled out of the parking lot without even looking at her, the sound of the motorcycle dying down to a faint buzz as he drove away from the school.

Jessica crossed her arms and fumed.

The following morning, Elizabeth stood in front of her opened locker, trying to get organized for her first period class. "What am I going to do?" she asked Maria, who was rummaging through her own locker a few feet away. "I can't think straight anymore. I hardly slept at all last night," Elizabeth admitted.

Maria closed her locker with a firm clang and leaned against it sideways, facing Elizabeth. "You're going to have to decide on your own," she said. "The only advice I have for you is to *be careful*. Guys like Todd don't come along every day, and he's bound to figure out sooner or later that your feelings for him have changed."

Elizabeth shut her locker and leaned forward, touching her forehead to the cool metal surface. "I think he already has." She felt Maria's hand on her arm.

"Elizabeth, you can't go on like this," Maria said. "You know that, don't you?"

Elizabeth turned around and nodded. "He caught me off guard yesterday at lunch when he asked me if I was keeping something from him. I didn't know what to say to him. Then when he called me last night, I told him I couldn't talk because I had too much homework to do."

Maria shook her head slowly. "You can't keep stringing him along. If I were you—"

"Hi, guys," Enid said brightly, interrupting the conversation. Her green eyes seemed radiant, and Elizabeth could tell she was excited about something.

It's just as well, Elizabeth thought wearily. So far, talking about her troubled feelings hadn't helped her one bit. She was still helplessly torn between her love for Todd and her unresolved attraction to Joey. "What's up?" she asked, welcoming the distraction.

Enid remained silent and glanced at Maria, obviously waiting for her to leave. Elizabeth frowned, irritated at Enid's rudeness.

But Maria seemed to take the hint good-naturedly. "I have some work to do in the *Oracle* office," she said, excusing herself graciously.

"I'll be along in a few minutes," Elizabeth told her.

"This is so incredible," Enid began when Maria was out of hearing range. "Have you met Jonathan Cain, the new student yet?"

"Sort of," Elizabeth grunted, thinking of Peggy Abbot's ruined history project. "What about him?"

Enid opened her locker and giggled. "I have no idea what books I need this morning."

Elizabeth eyed her suspiciously. "Enid, what's going on?"

"Jonathan Cain," she responded. "I'm so in love with him, I feel like my heart is as big as the whole world. Yesterday I was driving my mother's car to the store, listening to an old sappy song on the radio, and I just felt as if I were about to burst with joy. And then, the next thing I knew, I was crying."

Elizabeth frowned. "Are you sure there isn't something physically wrong with you?"

Enid laughed loudly, attracting a few curious glances. She ducked her head sheepishly and chuckled. "There I go again, bursting joyfully all over myself. Oh, Liz, you have to help me think of a way to meet him. Maybe we could plan an international awareness day and have him speak about his experience in other countries . . . or maybe we could walk by him and I'll pretend to fall and you ask him to carry me to the nurse's office."

Elizabeth blinked. *This is too weird,* she thought. *Enid is acting like one of Jessica's ditzy, boy-crazy friends!* "Enid, Jonathan Cain isn't your type," she said plainly. "He's rude and disgusting. And he's certainly not the hotshot Mr. Cooper made him out to be, believe me. Take my advice and stay away from that creep."

Enid's eyes flashed with anger. "Thanks a lot, Elizabeth," she spat out sarcastically. "I knew I could count on you to understand." She slammed her locker shut and strode away.

"Enid, come back here," Elizabeth called, immediately regretting having snapped at her best friend. But Enid kept going without a backward glance.

Elizabeth closed her eyes, feeling as if the ground beneath her feet were shifting, knocking her world off balance. *Something's wrong here,* she thought with gut certainty. *And it's going to get a whole lot worse.*

That afternoon Jessica skipped her French class again and headed out to the student parking lot during last period, armed with a brilliant new plan. She'd chosen her outfit carefully that morning—a deep purple miniskirt, topped with a lavender silk

T-shirt. Jessica considered purple to be a power color, and she was dressed for battle. A silver chain belt, which she'd borrowed from Lila ages ago, accentuated her slim waist. And a wide silver bracelet, also Lila's, showed off her perfectly manicured, deep rose fingernails.

Even after Jonathan had ignored her the day before, Jessica had never once considered giving up on him. *He will be mine,* she thought determinedly as she walked toward the Jeep.

When she and Elizabeth had arrived at school that morning, Jessica had parked in the spot where Jonathan had left his motorcycle the day before, hoping he'd choose the same area again. Elizabeth had looked at her as if she were crazy, but Jessica had retorted with Elizabeth's own smart-aleck answer from the previous morning: "I need the exercise."

Jessica was surprised when she spotted the Harley on the other side of the parking lot. *Is he trying to hide from me? Or is he just testing out the view from the various corners of the lot?* she mused, giggling. *If he's trying to hide from me, he can forget about it.*

Without hesitation, she hopped into the Jeep and drove over to Jonathan's Harley. *This is getting to be routine,* she thought as she pulled into the spot next to the motorcycle and shut off the motor.

Then, with a flick of her hand, she turned on the headlights.

She hopped out and looked around, pleased to see that there weren't any students in the area. "Fate is on my side," she whispered to herself as she tossed her keys in the air and caught them with one hand. The last thing she needed was a busybody do-gooder to come along and ruin everything.

Feeling very clever and giddy with excitement, Jessica sauntered back into the building.

Chapter 6

When Jessica returned to the Jeep after school, she made a halfhearted attempt to start the engine, checking to be sure the battery was dead. The Jeep responded with a clicking noise. "Surprise, surprise," Jessica mumbled wryly, containing her laughter.

She gave herself a mental pat on the back. *Well done!* she silently cheered as she grabbed her hairbrush for a quick touch-up.

"Engine trouble?" a male voice asked through the open window.

Startled, Jessica turned expectantly. But it was only Tim Nelson, a SVH football player, holding his chin as he studied her Jeep. "It's probably the battery," he suggested.

Well, isn't he brilliant? Jessica thought sarcastically.

71

Tim was an OK-looking guy and a pretty good football player. Normally she wouldn't have minded his attention. But that day she refused to put up with anyone who might interfere with her mission. She pushed open the car door, forcing him to step back. "I can handle it, Tim."

"I have jumper cables in my car," he told her.

"Good for you," she quipped.

"It wouldn't take much to get the engine started," he offered. "I'm parked in the next row."

Jessica rolled her eyes. "Thanks, but no thanks," she replied, anxious to get rid of him before Jonathan arrived. "I've got it completely under control." Tim finally got the message and walked away.

Jessica sashayed to the front of the Jeep and popped open the hood. Lounging against the fender, she watched the flow of students coming out the building and waited for her prey.

A few minutes later, Allen Walters, the *Oracle* photographer, and John Pfeifer, the sports editor, stopped by the Jeep, apparently trying to be gallant. "What seems to be the trouble?" Allen asked.

"Don't worry about it, guys," Jessica said in a breezy tone. "I'm sure you're on your way to cover some earth-shattering event."

John shook his head. "We have time to help you. It'll only take a minute to jump-start the engine."

"No, thanks," Jessica said firmly as she craned her neck to look over their shoulders. Jonathan was nowhere in sight.

Allen and John made no move to leave. Jessica rolled her eyes and exhaled loudly. "I don't need your help," she insisted in a gruff tone. The guys looked at each other and shrugged.

Jessica glared at them and waved. "Good-bye, guys. You have to go now."

They walked away, mumbling. Dismissing them from her mind, Jessica shifted to a more comfortable position against the fender and resumed her watch. Several more hopeful guys came up and asked if she wanted help, but she brushed them off quickly.

At last she spotted Jonathan ambling across the parking lot. Jessica noticed that several students—especially the girls—turned and stared at him. But Jonathan seemed oblivious to all the attention. *He's probably used to it,* Jessica thought. *A guy that hot must cause a sensation wherever he goes.*

She held her breath as he came closer. *Time for act two,* she told herself. She ducked her head under the hood and leaned over the engine, making sure that lots of leg showed. Her heart pounded as she waited for Jonathan's approach, positive that a beautiful romance was about to begin. *No guy can resist a girl in a miniskirt, especially if she's got car trouble,* she reassured herself. She could already hear the wedding bells. *I want a beach wedding, at sunset—*

Suddenly the loud noise of Jonathan's motorcycle blasted through Jessica's sweet fantasy. She looked up quickly, banging her head on the hood. Rubbing the sore spot, she whirled around. Her jaw dropped as she watched Jonathan peel out of the parking lot.

Frustrated, Jessica stamped her foot. *How dare he!* she thought hotly.

"I can't stop thinking about you-know-who's decision to transfer to UCLA so suddenly," Elizabeth admitted as she and Maria headed toward the exit. Their leisurely pace was at odds with the rushing river of students all around them.

"It does seem weird," Maria agreed. "When we were at camp, Jo—you-know-who told me the men in his family have been going to Yale for generations. And his mother went there for her master's degree."

Elizabeth nodded. Two freshman guys bumped into her, but she barely noticed. "I can understand his reasons," she said. "He wants to find his own way, and I respect him for that. It must have been a hard choice to make. Now he's out here, far from home. I'm sure he could use a good friend right now. Maybe I should just call—"

Maria stopped her with a direct, knowing look. "Nice try, Liz. But I'm afraid that excuse is as thin as slivered baloney. Joey is a friendly guy, and I'm sure he'll make plenty of friends at UCLA. If you're going to call him, at least be honest with yourself about the reason."

Elizabeth winced, as if she'd been jabbed. "You don't mince words, do you?"

Maria shrugged. "I'm a writer. I try to say it like I see it. Just like you."

Elizabeth sighed. "I know you're right."

They finally reached the front lobby, where the crowd had dispersed a bit. "Wouldn't you tell me the same thing if our situations were reversed?" Maria asked as she followed Elizabeth out the double doors.

Elizabeth noticed the subtle anxious look in Maria's eyes. She understood how risky it often felt to tell someone the truth—especially a friend. "I'd probably use a lot of the same words," Elizabeth said with a reassuring smile. "Although I doubt I'd ever be able to say 'thin as slivered baloney' without cracking up."

Maria sniffed, pretending to be highly insulted, then both of them laughed.

When they reached the student lot, Elizabeth saw that the spot where she and Jessica had parked that morning was empty. "Where's the Jeep?" she asked, frowning. "I can't figure out why Jessica keeps moving it."

"It's over there," Maria said, pointing to the other side of the lot.

Elizabeth raised her hand to her forehead to shield her eyes from the glare of the afternoon sun. The hood of the Jeep was up, and Jessica was leaning against the front fender with her arms crossed.

"Looks like you have car trouble," Maria remarked. "If it's just the battery, you're in luck. I have jumper cables in my trunk."

"Thanks." Elizabeth jogged across the lot to the Jeep while Maria went to get her car. "What's going on?" Elizabeth asked Jessica. "Won't it start?"

"The battery is dead," Jessica replied tersely.

"That's strange," Elizabeth said, bemused. "We didn't use the headlights this morning, and the battery is fairly new. I don't think we're due for a tune-up yet. . . ."

"Let's just get the stupid thing started and go home," Jessica grumbled.

Elizabeth nodded. "Maria has jumper cables."

As if on cue, Maria pulled up in her tan Mercedes, honking the horn. Within minutes, she'd connected the jumper cables between both car batteries and had the Jeep's engine started and idling smoothly.

Maria wound the jumper cables into a loose coil and put them back in the trunk of her car.

"Thanks, Maria," Elizabeth said.

Maria closed the trunk and brushed her hands together. "No problem. I used to have to start Nicole's car all the time. She drove a Volkswagen that was older than she was—with an even worse attitude, if you can believe it. It refused to start whenever the temperature dropped below freezing. And in New York, that happens a lot. I told Nicole there's no reason to have a car in Manhattan, but the girl absolutely refused to take the subway or a bus."

Elizabeth laughed, remembering Maria's friend who'd also been at Camp Echo Mountain with them. Nicole Banes had been one of the most mean-spirited, nasty, devious girls Elizabeth had ever met. But although they'd started out as archenemies, she and Elizabeth had become friends by the end of camp. "I wonder who's starting her car for her now?" Elizabeth said.

Maria laughed. "I just got a letter from her. It seems she's been getting rides to school from a hot guy in her honors history class."

Elizabeth smiled, genuinely pleased. "I'm glad to hear—"

"Come on, Liz, we have to go!" Jessica called.

"I'll be right there," Elizabeth answered, rolling her eyes. "I'll call you later, Maria. Thanks for helping us start the Jeep—and thanks for being a friend."

"Anytime," Maria replied.

Elizabeth waved to her and returned to the Jeep. Jessica was slumped down on the passenger side. "You drive," she said.

Elizabeth shrugged and pulled out her set of keys. As she drove through the familiar streets of Sweet Valley, she tried to imagine how Joey would see the passing scenery. Palm trees, bright sun, and balmy breezes meant home to her. She wondered if he missed the East Coast. *There I go again,* she thought sheepishly. *Will I ever get over him?*

"Jess, do you still think about Paul?" she asked hesitantly.

Jessica smiled. "Yeah, all the time. I don't think I would have gotten over Christian's death if it hadn't been for Paul."

Elizabeth nodded, remembering how worried she'd been about her twin. Jessica had sunk into a state of depression after her boyfriend Christian Gorman had drowned in Bruce Patman's pool during a gang fight.

"Paul and I had something special," Jessica added. "I don't think I'll ever forget him. Why do you ask?"

Elizabeth took a deep breath. "I got a letter from Joey a few days ago. It seems that when he got to Yale, he realized it was his parents' dream for him to be there, not his own. He's decided to transfer to UCLA, and he wants to see me again. It's so tempting," she admitted. "I wish I could put Joey out of my mind, but I can't." Elizabeth came to a smooth stop at a traffic light and turned to her sister. "I still have feelings for him."

"So what's the problem?" Jessica asked.

"Todd, my boyfriend. Remember him?" Elizabeth said.

Jessica shrugged. "Why not date both?"

Elizabeth shook her head, realizing that her twin would never understand. After all, she had started dating Christian while she was still going out with Ken Matthews, the captain of the SVH football team.

"I don't want to lose Todd," Elizabeth explained. "I'm already worried that my romance with Joey will get back to him. I'm sure Aaron and Winston suspect that there was something going on between Joey and me at camp—not to mention Lila, the queen of gossip."

Jessica giggled. "Don't worry about Lila. I'll take care of her. Her parents had a fit when those outrageous credit card charges began arriving from her stay at camp. I guess she set an all-time record for herself. She told them that she'd bought all that stuff for poor people who lived in a broken-down wooden shack near the camp. Gourmet food, fancy china, expensive sheets—can you imagine?"

Elizabeth smiled wryly. "Sounds like Lila. But what about the airplane she bought?" Lila and Bo had gotten lost in the woods and had used their credit cards to invest in a crop-dusting plane with the pilot who'd rescued them.

"Actually, that was the only bill Lila's parents didn't mind," Jessica replied. "But they'd have a fit if they found out that the only poor people in the woods Lila helped were herself and Bo. I'll just threaten to let them know if she tells anyone about you and Joey."

Elizabeth gulped and murmured, "Thanks." *Jessica is covering for me, and I'm encouraging her to blackmail her best friend?* she thought, shaking her head at the irony.

Jessica carried her lunch tray away from the food line the following day and scanned the tables in the cafeteria. *Jonathan has to come to lunch sooner or later,* she thought.

Lila came up behind her. "I wonder who you're looking for . . . a tall, dark stranger in tight black jeans, maybe?"

"Maybe," Jessica said over her shoulder. "And how do *you* know what kind of pants he's wearing today?" she asked suspiciously.

"I saw him in the hall after second period," Lila said.

Jessica turned around, intrigued. "Where, exactly? Was he alone? Did he say anything?"

Lila snorted. "Really, Jessica, how can you still be interested in that creep after he left you stranded with a dead battery yesterday afternoon?"

Jessica shrugged. "I've decided to give him another chance because I'm so generous. You should understand, after buying all that nice stuff for those poor people living in an old shack in the mountains back in Montana."

Lila giggled. "What can I say? I'm a creative genius."

Jessica smiled knowingly. "I just hope your parents never finds out."

A wary look crept into Lila's eyes. "Me too."

"I'm sure they won't," Jessica drawled innocently. "After all, I'm your best friend. You know I wouldn't breathe a word of it. And Elizabeth would never tell them, just like you'd never tell anyone about her and Joey, right?"

Lila squinted and pursed her lips, flashing Jessica a haughty look. Then she whirled around and stormed off in a huff.

Jessica watched her go, chuckling under her breath. *It's great to have a best friend who understands me so well,* she thought.

But where is Jonathan Cain? she wondered in frustration. She carried her lunch tray to the outdoor eating area and searched the picnic tables hopefully. Her heart did a somersault when she spotted a guy with dark hair, wearing black jeans and a black shirt, sitting with his back to her.

Without hesitation, she headed straight for him. But before she reached his table, the guy turned his head, and Jessica realized she'd been walking toward Roger Barrett Patman. *Darn!* she thought, scowling at Bruce's cousin. *How could I have mistaken Roger for Jonathan?* Grumbling, she went back inside and joined the crowd at her usual table, where Lila, Sandy, Amy, and Annie were already seated.

Jessica caught the nasty little gleam in Lila's eyes as she plunked her tray down on the table. *That's right, Lila, I didn't find Jonathan,* Jessica thought, sending her a dirty look in return. *Having a best friend who understands me so well can also be a pain,* she realized.

Jessica ripped open a cellophane package of chocolate chip cookies just as Heather Mallone arrived. "Jessica Wakefield, those are full of sugar, and do you *know* how many fat grams there are in a single cookie?"

Jessica raised one eyebrow. "And do I care?"

Heather flipped her hair back and exhaled

loudly. "As cocaptains of the cheerleading squad, you and I should be setting a good example for the other girls on the squad."

"Moderation, variety, and balance are the keys to a healthy diet," Jessica proclaimed, paraphrasing an article she'd read in *Cheerleading* magazine. She'd made a habit of studying each issue, arming herself with knowledge to use against Heather's know-it-all attitude.

Heather looked as if she were trying to think of a comeback when Caroline Pearce came over to their table and sat down, her whole face radiating with excitement. Jessica knew there was only one thing that could energize Caroline like that—gossip. She was the biggest gossip in Sweet Valley High, beating Lila by far.

"Has anyone met the new guy yet?" Caroline asked.

Lila glanced at Jessica, then turned to Caroline with a wide-eyed, innocent look. "Why do you ask?"

"Well," Caroline said, her green eyes twinkling, "I heard some of the teachers talking about him when I was walking by the faculty lounge."

"With your ear pressed against the door," Jessica quipped. Amy giggled.

Caroline shot Jessica a dirty look before continuing. "It seems that Jonathan Cain is taking advanced chemistry, and I heard Mr. Russo saying that he offered to excuse Jonathan from the unit exam this morning because he'd only been in the class for a few days. But Jonathan insisted on taking it. And he aced it!"

Caroline paused and took a long drink of her fruit punch, an action that Jessica recognized as a dramatic ploy.

"Who would have guessed that he was the nerdy type?" Lila said, directing the comment at Jessica.

Jessica smiled wryly. "You mean like Bo?"

Lila tossed a candy wrapper at her. "Watch your mouth, Wakefield."

"And then," Caroline said, dabbing her lips with a paper napkin, "Ms. Jacobi said that she was shocked when she corrected Jonathan's homework, because he seems to know more about modern cultures of Eastern Europe than she does. She was in the library for hours last night, looking up the stuff he'd written in his essay. And all of his information was accurate."

"I *thought* there was something weird about him," Amy interjected. "Besides the way he looks and dresses, I mean. Although I have to admit he's pretty hot. He walked by me in the hall this morning, and I felt tingly all over, you know?"

A few of the girls laughed. "I guess he's OK,"

Sandy agreed. "If you like that pale-skinned type."

"It looks like a few others think he's hot too," Amy said, gesturing to a table behind Jessica. "Check out the gothic gang."

Jessica turned and saw a group of girls dressed in dramatic black and white, with reddish black lipstick and heavy black eyeliner. *They're obviously hoping to attract Jonathan's attention,* she thought.

Lila shuddered. "Talk about fashion misfits!"

"They're such misguided amateurs," Jessica scoffed. "They don't stand a chance with him." She glanced across the table and saw the open curiosity on Caroline's face.

I'd better reserve my triumph, especially since I've yet to talk to the slippery guy, Jessica realized. *But when I do . . .* She giggled, sure that Jonathan was going to find himself wrapped around her finger very soon.

Jessica ducked into the girls' room before the start of last period. Brushing her hair in front of the mirror, she considered her next move. *Maybe I should go out there and chain Jonathan's Harley to the Jeep,* she thought, *and let the air out of our tires.* It would certainly prevent him from rushing off without speaking to her.

For a moment she wondered if she might find a metal chain in the industrial arts department. Then she burst out laughing, imagining herself pulling such a bizarre trick. Maybe when she and Jonathan finally got together, she'd tell him how close she'd come to criminal vandalism.

When the bell rang a few seconds later, she still hadn't come up with anything halfway decent. Frustrated, she tossed her hairbrush into her backpack. "I may as well take the afternoon off and go to class," she grumbled under her breath.

She slipped into her French class and grabbed a seat just as the second bell rang. As she pulled her book out of her bag, she glanced at the student in the seat beside her.

Jessica's heart skipped a beat, and the textbook dropped to the floor. She was sitting right next to Jonathan Cain.

Yes! she mentally cheered as she bent over to pick up her book. *If this isn't destiny, I don't know what is.*

Ms. Dalton began the class as she always did. "*Bonjour, mes amis,*" she said, wishing a good day to her "friends" in a voice that was bubbling with enthusiasm. She was fairly pretty for a teacher, with straight dark hair and hazel eyes.

Jessica wondered if Jonathan found Ms. Dalton attractive, but she quickly dismissed the pesky idea. *Jonathan is my destiny,* she thought confidently.

As Ms. Dalton began a review of French irregular verbs, Jessica glanced at Jonathan. He was staring straight ahead, not really looking at anyone. She wasn't fooled. *He's aware of me as much as I am of him,* she thought.

Ms. Dalton conjugated some new verbs on the chalkboard, and everyone took out their notebooks. Jessica pulled out hers too. But instead of taking down French notes, she wrote, *"So tell me, Jonathan Cain, do you always ignore damsels in distress, or were you just feeling rude yesterday?"*

Grinning mischievously, she ripped the page out and folded it in half. When Ms. Dalton's back was turned, she tossed it onto Jonathan's desk.

At first he ignored the note. Jessica tapped her fingernails on her book, waiting. Finally he picked it up and unfolded it. Jessica's heart beat rapidly as she watched him reading. Then he quickly wrote something in the space below her message and returned the note to her desk.

Jessica's hands trembled as she read his response. *You don't want to mess with me,* it said. *I eat little girls like you for breakfast.*

A sharp thrill shot up and down Jessica's spine. Thoroughly intrigued, she licked her lips and flashed him a sexy smile. He kept his eyes forward, but Jessica wasn't the least bit discouraged. She loved a challenge. *You can try to ignore me all you want, but I know you feel the electric connection between us,* she thought.

Everything about him was gorgeous. Ignoring the French lesson, Jessica spent the class studying her destiny. He was wearing a tight black T-shirt that showed off the smooth lines of his muscular arms. His right hand was resting on the open page of his French book. Jessica imagined his long, graceful fingers entwined with hers. . . .

Her gaze fell on the ornate ring he wore on his middle finger. It appeared to be carved from wood, inlaid with silver and onyx. *Someday he'll take that ring off and give it to me,* she vowed.

Chapter 7

Maria lay back on the velvet-covered chaise longue in Elizabeth's room the following evening and continued with the story of her life. "After the Crystal Drops shampoo commercials, I got my first movie role, Jannie in *The Visitor*. It was hard because they shot the movie on location in Canada, which meant having to be away from home for weeks at time. I was lucky because my parents took turns staying with me.

"I was all set to do another science fiction movie after that, but the project was canceled and I became the Princess Macaroni girl. Then I did commercials for Feathersoft, where I got to dress up like a giant roll of toilet paper. It could have been lots of fun, but the wardrobe lady was mean. I remember one afternoon when

89

she started yelling at me and her face turned red—"

Maria stopped suddenly and giggled. "Elizabeth, I can't believe I've been talking about myself for nearly two hours and I still haven't gotten into the teen years. You must be running out of disk space by now."

Sitting at her desk, Elizabeth stared at the gibberish on the screen of her laptop computer and cringed. She'd invited Maria over so that they could go over the details of her background for the "Personal Profiles" column, which was due the following day. But Elizabeth still hadn't managed to type a coherent sentence.

Maria got up and peered over Elizabeth's shoulder. "'Joey green eyes, Todd brown eyes, Joey lake, Todd ocean, Joey mountains, Todd beaches . . .' What is that?" Maria asked.

Elizabeth's face grew hot. "I'm sorry. I just can't seem to think tonight."

Maria smiled wryly, shaking her head. "No, the problem is that you can't *stop* thinking."

Elizabeth sighed. No matter how hard she'd tried to concentrate on Maria's interview, her mind had constantly wandered back to her guy problems. "I'm obsessing, aren't I?" she admitted weakly.

Maria nodded. "*Obsessing*. That's the word I

would use too," she replied matter-of-factly. "I think it's time for a break. Let's go for a swim."

"I feel terrible about wasting your time like this," Elizabeth said, pushing back her chair.

Maria waved as if to brush away the apology. "Don't mention it. Let me borrow a swimsuit and I'll even restrain myself from calling you 'Dizzy Lizzie,'" she teased, referring to the nickname given to Elizabeth by the bratty ten-year-old girls in the group she'd been assigned at Camp Echo Mountain.

"You're terrible," Elizabeth retorted. Chuckling in spite of herself, she tossed a pillow in the general direction of Maria's head.

"Yes, Lila, he did it again." Jessica shifted the phone to her other ear and reached for the bottle of lavender nail polish on her bedside table, accidentally knocking an empty root beer can and several CDs to the floor. Oblivious to the mess, she continued, "Today I left my French book in my locker so that I'd have to share with him during class."

"Nice idea," Lila said. "Simple but direct. So what happened?"

Clutching the phone to her ear with her shoulder, Jessica unscrewed the top of the bottle of nail polish. "Ms. Dalton showed a dumb movie about the wine and cheese industries in southern France," she said as she began polishing her nails.

"Bo's relatives on his mother's side own a vineyard in France. Did I tell you that?" Lila asked.

Jessica grunted. "Yes, at least a million times."

Lila sighed over the line. "French culture is so romantic. Maybe you should start writing French love letters to Jonathan," she suggested. "Bo wrote me a poem."

Jessica paused with the nail polish brush in midair. "If you start reading it over the phone, I'm hanging up."

Lila laughed. "Don't worry. I don't think you could handle it."

"Very funny." Jessica held her hand out a few feet in front of her face, admiring her handiwork before moving on to her other hand. "What do you think of that black nail polish everyone is wearing at school?" she asked.

"It's gross, and I don't—" A call-waiting click sounded on Lila's line. "Hold on, Jess. And hope it's Bo."

Jessica rolled her eyes and finished polishing her fingernails, then moved on to her toenails as she continued waiting for Lila to return. After she'd finished applying a second coat, Jessica gave up and carefully replaced the phone receiver. She would have slammed it, but she didn't want to mess up her nails. "Some friend you are, Lila," she grumbled.

A second later the phone rang again. Jessica picked it up, prepared to give Lila a piece of her mind. But it was Enid calling for Elizabeth. Disappointed, Jessica hollered for her sister. When Elizabeth didn't answer, Jessica considered the painstaking work she'd done on her nails, which still hadn't dried, and decided to take a message.

Forcing herself to concentrate on nothing more than the rhythm of her breathing and the motion of her limbs, Elizabeth swam lap after lap in her family's backyard pool, long after Maria had quit.

Thoroughly exhausted, Elizabeth finally dragged herself over to the edge. Her muscles felt like boiled macaroni as she lifted herself out of the pool.

Maria was lounging in a chair near the pool, reading one of Jessica's magazines. "Here's your answer, Liz," she said. "'How to Keep Your Man in the Dark: Do's and Don'ts that Really Work.' This article is great. Listen—'Rule number one: don't tell,'" she read aloud. "'Remember, everything you say can be used against you. The dirty secret you want to get off your chest may be shot back at you as a poison arrow.'"

Elizabeth grabbed her towel from a nearby chair and wrapped it around her hair, turban style. "Keep going," she told Maria.

"'Rule number two: Don't forget that honesty is the best policy—eighty percent of the time. Truthful details can cloud even a mountain of a lie.'" Maria read silently for a few seconds, then whistled. "'For instance, do tell your guy that you ran into his best friend last Saturday night—don't tell him that it was a lip-to-lip encounter.' Wow!" Maria exclaimed. "Someone has put a lot of thought into this."

Elizabeth shook her head. "I couldn't do it. I guess I'm just not made for deception."

Maria looked up and smiled. "The Elizabeth Wakefield I knew back in middle school certainly wasn't. I'm glad some things haven't changed."

Elizabeth plopped down in a chair next to Maria and closed her eyes. "I remember when Jessica was cheating on Ken Matthews with Christian Gorman from Palisades," she said. "I didn't understand how she could hurt Ken like that or risk all they had together for a guy she'd just met." Elizabeth opened her eyes and turned to Maria. "Now I do."

"And what do you plan to do about it?" Maria asked.

Elizabeth looked up at the sky. "Weren't the stars in Montana something?" she murmured, comparing her view with the night sky at Camp Echo Mountain.

"Yes. But I'm not letting you change the subject," Maria replied pointedly.

Elizabeth exhaled loudly. "I know what I have to do. I knew it back at camp when I told Joey good-bye. Now I have to say good-bye to him all over again. And again, it hurts."

"But it's for the best," Maria reminded her.

Elizabeth murmured in agreement, trying to feel confident in her decision. The letter had thrown her into a state of confusion. *The letter!* she realized.

She jumped up and headed back into the house. "I'll be right back," she called to Maria over her shoulder. Forcing herself not to think, Elizabeth ran upstairs to her room.

Less than a minute later, she returned to the patio, clutching Joey's letter to her chest. *I have to do this,* she told herself as she laid the letter, still in its envelope, on the Wakefields' barbecue grill.

A chair scraped against the patio as Maria got up and walked over to the grill. Elizabeth glanced at her friend. Maria nodded.

Elizabeth took a deep breath and struck a match. With her hand trembling, she lowered the flaming tip to the edge of the white envelope. "I hereby commit Joey Mason's memory to ashes," she announced solemnly.

"And I'm the witness," Maria said softly.

Elizabeth watched the flame take hold, curling the corner of Joey's personalized stationery. She felt a sharp pang as she watched the fire obliterate his handwriting. She brushed away a tear, then felt Maria's hand on her shoulder.

"It's OK, Elizabeth," Maria whispered. "This was the right thing to do."

Elizabeth nodded. Even in her sadness, she felt as though a great burden had been lifted off her shoulders.

As they stood over the dying embers, Jessica opened the sliding glass patio door. "Here you are," she said. "Are you guys roasting marshmallows or something?"

"Not exactly," Elizabeth answered, watching as flecks of the charred letter floated away.

"Enid called earlier," Jessica told her.

Elizabeth was making a mental note to call Enid back when the portable phone on the patio table suddenly rang. "That's probably her now," she mumbled as she absently answered it.

But when Elizabeth heard the caller's voice, her heart skipped a beat. "Hello, Todd. I'm glad you called."

Her eyes met Maria's. Maria gave Elizabeth a thumbs-up sign and went into the house.

Todd gripped the phone so hard, his fingers were turning white. "Elizabeth, I can't keep going on like this. I know there's something wrong. We have to get together and talk." *Get ready for another one of her flimsy excuses*, he told himself.

"I agree," Elizabeth said, throwing him off balance.

He swallowed hard. He was surprised that Elizabeth had agreed to see him so quickly—and he was worried.

"You do?"

"Do you want to come over now?" she asked.

"Oh . . . um . . . sure," Todd said hesitantly. "Yeah, sure. I'll be there in a few minutes. Maybe we could go for a drive or something."

"That sounds wonderful," she replied.

Elizabeth disconnected the call with a soft click that sounded so final. Todd stared at the phone receiver in his hand for a long time. He finally slammed it down when a recorded voice came over the line telling him the phone was off the hook.

Bracing his elbows on his knees, Todd hung his head. *Elizabeth is going to dump me*, he thought.

❖   ❖   ❖

Todd's hands were cold, but his palms were sweaty as he turned onto Calico Drive. Elizabeth was in the front yard and Maria Slater's tan Mercedes was pulling out of the Wakefields' driveway just as Todd arrived. Elizabeth waved goodbye to Maria, then came bounding across the front yard to his car. *Is she excited to see me or in a hurry to dump me?* he wondered.

"I'm glad you called, Todd," she said softly as she pulled the seat belt across her shoulder.

Todd glanced at her, trying to read the look on her face, but all he could think about was how pretty she was. Her eyes were bright and her lips seemed so soft. . . . Tearing his gaze away with a silent moan, he faced front and pulled away from the curb.

They drove to Secca Lake in silence. Todd took the unpaved road around the lake, thinking of all the great times he and Elizabeth had shared at the scenic spot. *Are they about to become ancient history?* he wondered sadly.

He reached the end of the road and parked near the abandoned boathouse. Finally he and Elizabeth would have a chance to talk without being disturbed.

Todd hung his arms loosely on the steering wheel and stared into the darkness. Next to him, he heard Elizabeth sigh.

What exactly is going on in her head? he asked himself. The tension in the car was gnawing at his gut. Even if the truth would hurt, he had to know.

"Elizabeth?" he whispered, turning to her. But before he could get another word out, she wrapped her arms around his neck and kissed him as he had never been kissed before.

Todd's doubts and fears melted away as he held her in his arms, letting himself get lost in the sweet moment. It was obvious to him that despite whatever had been bothering her, their relationship was back on solid ground. Elizabeth seemed more in love with him than ever.

"The first European women to survive in the New World arrived in Jamestown in 1619." Mr. Fellows paused to pull down a large map at the front of the room.

How would I look with black hair like Jonathan's? Enid wondered, half dozing as the history lecture continued. She'd been doodling in her notebook all period to stay awake.

U.S. History was her last class of a long, tiring day. The night before, Enid had dreamed that she and Jonathan had driven to Miller's Point and he'd built her a castle there, turning Sweet Valley's most popular parking spot into a secluded romantic hideaway just for her.

". . . within seventy-two hours of their arrival, all the women had married, thereby establishing families and giving England a strong foothold in the Americas," Mr. Fellows droned on, pulling down a second map. "Let's compare this to Spain's . . ."

Enid sighed, imagining herself on a huge ship like those early women, sailing to a distant land to find her true love, and then seeing Jonathan standing on the shore. *The ship is filled with beautiful young women, but Jonathan sees only me, his gleaming blue eyes capturing me with their sexy, mesmerizing light, his black hair ruffled by the wind. He waits, and when we finally reach each other* . . .

"Ms. Rollins, would it trouble you to pass in your paper?" Mr. Fellows demanded.

Enid looked up and saw her history teacher standing next to her seat with his arms folded, glaring down at her. It took her a few seconds to figure out that he was referring to the class's assignment.

Enid's face grew hot. "I didn't get it finished," she mumbled. Mr. Fellows frowned and walked away.

Enid had been too busy to do homework the night before. She'd spent the entire evening imagining the house she and Jonathan would live in someday.

Remembering, Enid sighed dreamily. *Our house is going to be elegant and chic, with leather furniture, a big fireplace, soft rugs—*

The dismissal bell rang, startling her.

"Be sure to go over today's notes for the test on Monday," Mr. Fellows announced, raising his voice over the scraping of chairs and slamming of books.

Enid looked down at her notebook and read what she'd written among the hearts and flowers. *E.R. loves J.C. . . . Enid Rollins Cain . . . Enid Alexandra Cain . . .* She sighed. *I used to be concerned about stuff like history tests,* she thought blandly.

But now she had other, more important things on her mind. And her top priority was getting Jonathan's attention. *I'm ready to do something drastic,* Enid decided excitedly. She hurried to find Elizabeth, anxious to tell her about the plan.

Enid found Elizabeth in the *Oracle* office, where she and Maria were engaged in another one of their whispering conferences. Enid strolled into the room too excited to let it bother her. "Guess what, Liz," she said brightly.

Elizabeth looked up with a blank expression. "Oh, hi, Enid. What's up? I'm sorry I didn't call you back last night, but things are so crazy right now. I was up late finishing my column for the *Oracle*."

Enid waved aside the apology. "That's OK. Anyway, listen to this—I'm thinking of dyeing my hair black. Want to go with me to the salon in the mall this afternoon, before I lose my nerve?"

Elizabeth and Maria stared at her as if she were crazy. "What's wrong?" Enid asked.

"I think that's the stupidest idea I've ever heard," Elizabeth replied. "Why would you want to do something so ridiculous?"

Enid winced as if she'd been slapped. "What's so ridiculous about wanting a change?"

Elizabeth rolled her eyes and glanced at Maria. "What do you think?"

"I'm not sure if black hair will do much for your skin tone," Maria said, shaking her head.

Enid looked down and shrugged, too hurt to reply.

"I agree with Maria," Elizabeth said. "I don't think black hair would look good on you at all."

"In *your* opinion," Enid shot back.

Elizabeth nodded. "That's right. In our honest opinion."

"One hundred percent honesty, not eighty percent," Maria mumbled.

Enid frowned, confused. She had no idea what

Maria meant. But apparently Elizabeth did, because she closed her eyes and groaned, as if Maria had just told a bad joke.

Enid felt totally left out as she watched them exchange meaningful looks. *Thanks for the support, best friend,* Enid thought sarcastically as she withdrew from Elizabeth and stalked out of the room.

Chapter 8

"We're trying to get that new guy, Jonathan, to join the basketball team," Todd told Elizabeth as they walked hand in hand along the beach later that afternoon. Cool sea foam lapped over their bare feet, and seagulls circled overhead, their cries carried by the wind. The sun was just beginning to set, sending streaks of pink and pale orange across the sky and water.

Elizabeth gazed out over the horizon, frowning. She'd suggested driving to the beach after school in the hope that the setting would inspire romantic feelings for Todd in her. But so far it hadn't worked. His constant harping about the "magnificent" Jonathan Cain wasn't helping either.

Todd let go of her hand and bent down to pick up a pebble. "I saw him yesterday in the gym, shooting baskets. He's something else."

Elizabeth groaned to herself and tried to change the subject. "I turned in my column about Maria today and decided to do a follow-up article about child actors. Some of the stories she told me were fascinating."

"Jonathan didn't miss one shot, even from clear across the gym. I've never seen anything like it," Todd declared, flinging the rock into the ocean.

Elizabeth clenched her jaw and exhaled loudly. "That's so nice, Todd," she replied sarcastically.

He grabbed her hand and gave her a sheepish look. "There I go again, rambling on and on about basketball."

"It's OK, really," Elizabeth said with a sigh. "I should be used to it by now—love you, love your sport."

Todd chuckled and hugged her to his side. "You're more important to me than basketball, Liz. Didn't I prove it to you when I drove all the way up to Montana just to spend the weekend with you at Camp Echo Mountain?"

Elizabeth nodded, suddenly contrite. *I'm not being fair to Todd,* she realized. He had been making an effort, while she had concentrated on finding fault with him. *That's all going to change right now,* she vowed. Pushing everything else out of her mind except Todd, she wrapped her arms around his neck and pressed her lips to his for a deep, lingering kiss.

"I'll take a bottle of Midnight Song nail polish," Enid said as she handed the color chart back to the manicurist. The petite woman nodded curtly as she arranged various bottles, tubes, and jars on the small table between them.

Enid's visit to the salon was turning out to be a fabulous adventure. She had decided to treat herself to a whole beauty makeover instead of just a new hairstyle.

A solid line of mirrors ran the entire length of the salon, making the space seem infinitely wide and bright. Enid glanced at her reflection and grinned, pleased at what she saw. The girl looking back at her was nothing like the old Enid. *My entire life is about to change, so why shouldn't my looks?* she reasoned. *Jonathan is worth it.*

Her formerly curly reddish brown hair had been chemically straightened and dyed black. Enid turned her head slightly, loving the way it cascaded down her back. Straightening it had made it seem much longer.

Her face was different too. Her eyebrows had been plucked to thin, glamorous arcs. Her complexion was rosy and smooth; a thick green mint-scented facial mask had left her pores deep-cleansed and tight. And now her hands were being exfoliated, massaged, and creamed.

The manicurist instructed Enid to soak her hands in a basin of warm, rose-scented water. A few minutes later a young assistant brought over a fluffy, heated towel. Enid felt as if she were resting in a cloud of luxury as she dried her soft, velvety smooth hands.

She watched in awe as long, tapered acrylic fingernails were applied over her short, stubby ones. After shaping them meticulously, the manicurist brushed each nail with several coats of shiny black polish.

The result was breathtaking. Enid held her hands out at arm's length. Moving her fingers slightly, she marveled at the play of reflected light shimmering across her glamorous nails. *Amazing!* she thought.

When her nails had dried completely, Enid spent some time in consultation with the salon's cosmetologist. The statuesque woman's brown eyes sparkled with enthusiasm as she demonstrated her newest color collection. Enid described what she wanted and put herself in the expert's hands.

The beautician hummed as she dabbed and brushed liquids, powders, and creams on Enid's face. "You're going for a very popular look, dear. And with your clear, young-looking complexion, anything goes."

The woman stroked a thin, wet brush along the edge of Enid's eyelids, ending with a tickling swirl in the outer corners. "OK, you can peek now," she said.

Enid opened her eyes and looked in the mirror. "I can't believe it's me!" she exclaimed.

"Beauty is a simple matter if you use quality products," the beautician said proudly. "Our new line of makeup is foolproof. And our skin care regime, used twice daily, can keep your complexion fresh and young-looking for many years to come." The woman punctuated her words with a huge grin.

When Enid finally left the salon, her cash was completely gone, but her heart was brimming with self-confidence. *Wait until Jonathan sees me,* she mused, imagining the look of adoration on his gorgeous face. She was sure that he would finally notice her and recognize the special bond between them.

"Enid," a voice called from behind, "is that you?" Enid turned and saw Maria Slater rushing over to her. *My favorite person in the world,* Enid thought bitterly.

"You really did it!" Maria exclaimed.

Enid glanced over Maria's shoulder with an obviously uninterested expression. "Do you mind? I'm really in a hurry."

Maria didn't seem to catch the hint. "I wasn't even sure it was you, Enid. You look so—different. But it's pretty. I like it."

Enid flashed her a tight, snide grin. "What a relief," she retorted sarcastically. "The glamour queen of Hollywood, New York, and Sweet Valley likes the way *I* look. Thank you so much, Maria. I probably would have died without your approval."

Maria's smile dropped, and a wounded look came into her eyes. Enid raised her chin defiantly and realized that she didn't care if her behavior had hurt Maria. *I'm sick of worrying about everyone else's feelings,* she thought angrily as she walked away. *No one ever worries about mine.*

As Elizabeth walked by the *Oracle* office on Monday morning, Maria popped her head out the door. "I need your help, Liz, quick. It's an emergency."

"What's the matter?" Elizabeth asked, startled. It was nearly an hour before first period, and the halls were still empty and quiet.

"I'm sorry if I frightened you, but I'm going crazy." Maria reached up and grabbed handfuls of her short, curly hair, as if to prove the point. "I just finished an article about the music company my mother works for, and I can't tell if it's the best thing I've ever written or if it stinks like old fish guts. I want you to read it and tell me the honest truth. I'm just printing it out now."

Elizabeth chuckled. "Are we talking about eighty percent truth or one hundred percent?"

"That depends on whether you like the article or not," Maria replied.

Elizabeth could see that her friend was really concerned, in spite of the joking. "I doubt it smells like old fish," she assured Maria, "but I'll be right back. I have to go to my locker."

"OK, but hurry!" Maria said dramatically.

Elizabeth was still smiling as she spun her locker combination. She felt better than she had in weeks. Jessica was planning to ride to school with Lila that morning, so Elizabeth had taken the opportunity to come in early to work on her article for the *Oracle*. She was pleased that Maria had done the same.

Burning Joey's note was the right thing to do, Elizabeth thought. Finally she felt free to concentrate on her work and her friends. And she was convinced that her relationship with Todd was on firm ground at last. She'd spent a lot of time with him over the weekend. When he'd kissed her at Miller's Point on Saturday night, Elizabeth had felt some of the old spark returning to her heart.

She absently opened her locker, then jumped back as a wooden canoe paddle suddenly fell out and crashed to the floor. The sound echoed in the empty hallway.

"What the—" Elizabeth knelt down and picked it up, her heart racing.

The paddle had been polished to a glossy sheen and decorated with colorful drawings depicting the various sites at Camp Echo Mountain—the main lodge, with gray smudges curling above its three chimneys, kidney-shaped Lake Vermillion, and Echo Mountain itself, its peak rising into a cloud. Between the drawings were appliqués of the camp flag and insignia.

Elizabeth was sure Joey had left the paddle in her locker. *He was here,* she realized. *Joey was actually in Sweet Valley High, in my locker! When?*

She tried to deny to herself that she felt a thrill, even though her hands were trembling as she tucked the paddle back into her locker.

Elizabeth thought about Joey all morning. By lunchtime her mind was reeling with questions. *How did he know which locker was mine?* she wondered as she walked into the noisy cafeteria. She took her place in the food line and absently picked up a clean tray from the stack at the end of the counter. *How did he manage to open my locker?* she asked herself. She knew that the doors locked automatically when they were shut. *Did one of the maintenance workers open it for him? Over the weekend?* She figured Joey had probably come to the school on Friday afternoon.

Two freshman girls got in line behind her, distracting Elizabeth with their bubbling chatter. "Have you seen the hand-painted black dresses at Blue Parrot Crafts?" one of the girls asked her friend. "They're so vampy!"

"Let's go shopping after school," the other said. "I want to buy some hair color. My mother finally agreed to let me dye my hair black. Of course, she thinks I'm only going to put a dark rinse in it, but I'm planning to use the permanent kind—*by mistake,* of course." Both girls giggled.

Elizabeth rolled her eyes as she selected a carton of lemon yogurt and a tossed salad from the food counter. *It seems the black head-to-toe look is catching on at SVH,* she thought wryly.

She moved away from the line and scanned the cafeteria tables, looking for Todd. Bruce Patman, Barry Rork, and Kirk Anderson were sitting at a nearby table, all three dressed in black. Elizabeth shook her head, somewhat amused.

She spotted Todd sitting with Winston and Maria Santelli. As Elizabeth approached their table, she noticed that Todd was also wearing black jeans and a black T-shirt, the new gothic "uniform." *Not him too,* she thought in dismay.

"Don't you look vampy," Elizabeth teased as she sat next to Todd.

Winston was also wearing black, but with a huge fluorescent green polka-dot tie. "What about me?" he asked eagerly.

Elizabeth shook her head, laughing. "You are beyond description, Winston."

Winston beamed proudly.

"I bought him the tie," Maria said, "so I can tell him apart from the crowd."

Elizabeth glanced at Todd and saw that he was scowling at her. "What's wrong with the way I look?" he asked defensively.

Elizabeth raised her eyebrows. "Nothing—if you're trying to copy Jonathan Cain."

"I'm not trying to *copy* him," Todd argued. "I just think he's cool. And what's wrong with what I'm wearing?"

Elizabeth shrugged. "Never mind," she said. Todd mumbled something incoherent.

Maria Slater came over to their table and joined them. "The two lovely Marias," Winston quipped. His girlfriend gave him a withering look.

"We do have to figure out a way to keep you guys straight," Elizabeth said.

Maria Slater laughed. "So long as you don't start calling us 'black Maria' and 'white Maria.'"

"I second that," Maria Santelli interjected.

"We'll just have to call you by your last names," Winston declared.

Maria Slater and Elizabeth looked at each other and blurted out, "Buford and Johansen." Everyone laughed, except Todd.

"They're talking about two guys from Camp Echo Mountain," Maria Santelli explained to Todd. "Buford and Johansen were best friends from Philadelphia. Both of them were named Steven, so everyone called them by their last names."

"Even their own mothers," Maria Slater added.

"Hey, I *visited* Camp Echo Mountain," Todd reminded them. "And I even met Buford and Johansen. But I still don't see what's so funny."

Maria Santelli smiled. "You should have read Winston's letters from camp. Buford and Johansen were his heroes."

Winston sighed dramatically. "I loved those two guys. They were really special."

"That's one word to describe them," Maria Slater said.

Winston raised his eyebrows, glowering. "Hey, it's not every day I meet guys who are nerdier than me." Again everyone laughed, except Todd.

Elizabeth sighed. Talking about camp brought back the bittersweet memories that were never far from her mind. Once again her thoughts turned to Joey. It couldn't have been easy for him to give up

Yale, but he had to in order to find his own way in life instead of living his parents' dream.

Elizabeth looked at Todd and tried to feel in love with him, but she couldn't seem to get past his scowling expression and ridiculous outfit. *Joey would never fall prey to trends*, she told herself.

At the *Oracle* staff meeting after school, Maria held her breath, waiting anxiously to hear what everyone thought about the article she'd written— her first for the *Oracle*. She studied their faces as they read the copies she'd passed out, hoping to gauge their reactions.

Olivia Davidson, the arts editor, pushed back her frizzy brown hair as her gaze flickered across the page. Maria stared absently at the green feather hanging from Olivia's earring. *Maybe I should have punched up the middle paragraphs a bit more*, Maria thought, twirling a pencil in her fingers nervously.

She glanced at Elizabeth, who smiled back reassuringly. Elizabeth had already told her the article was wonderful, but Maria wanted to know if it would also rate as highly with people who weren't her close friends.

John Pfeifer raised his head and nodded. "It's good—descriptive but concise."

"Oops," Olivia said as she marked her copy

with her pencil. "Typo on the last page."

Maria frowned and flipped to the last page. "Oh, I see," she said, grimacing. She'd written *herd* instead of *heard*.

"But other than that, I'd say it's perfect," Olivia said.

Penny Ayala, the editor, nodded. "I agree. And it's a good tie-in with Elizabeth's story about you in the 'Personal Profiles' column."

The others had similar comments. Maria smiled brightly, unabashedly basking in the praise.

"So it looks like this issue of the *Oracle* is all set," Penny announced. "And for the next issue, we'll have John's coverage of the San Pedro High game, Olivia's piece about the watercolor exhibition at the civic center . . . Elizabeth, have you picked someone for your next column?"

Before Elizabeth could say anything, Allen Walters glanced at Maria and shook his head, chuckling. "Maria Slater is a tough act to follow. I think she's ruined it for everyone else. Maybe we should scrap the 'Personal Profiles' column altogether," he joked.

A warm glow came over Maria. Working on the *Oracle* meant a lot to her. Receiving praise for her writing was wonderful, but being teased at a staff meeting made her feel that she was really part of the gang.

She flashed Allen a flirty smile and batted her lashes. "Thanks. I didn't know you cared," she purred dramatically. Everyone laughed.

"What about Jonathan Cain?" Olivia suggested. "He's certainly newsworthy." The others seemed to agree. Maria wasn't too crazy about him; something about him made her feel uneasy. But Olivia was right—he had been generating a lot of interest with the students since his arrival at SVH.

Elizabeth's face turned pale. "Well—" She gulped and looked around the room as if she were stalling for time. "I don't know if he's giving interviews."

Huh? Maria frowned, wondering what was going on in Elizabeth's head.

"It's worth a try, Elizabeth," Penny said.

"I'll think about it," Elizabeth mumbled unconvincingly.

When the meeting was over, Maria caught up with Elizabeth at her locker. But before she could ask Elizabeth about her strange behavior during the *Oracle* meeting, Maria noticed a canoe paddle in her friend's locker. "What is that?" she asked.

Elizabeth let out a shaky breath and took the paddle out of her locker. "I found it here this morning."

Maria studied the colorful markings. "Who is it from? Was there a note or anything?"

118

Elizabeth shook her head. "I don't need a note to know who it's from."

"Joey," Maria whispered.

"I'm pretty sure it was him," Elizabeth said. "And I'm more confused than ever."

Maria raised her eyebrows. "It's going to be a lot harder to burn *that*. I don't think it'll fit on your barbecue grill.".

Elizabeth gasped, as if Maria had suggested something criminal.

"I'm sorry," Maria said softly. "That was a mean thing for me to say."

Elizabeth pulled a few books out of her locker and slammed the door shut. "I don't want to talk about Joey."

"OK, let's talk about the *Oracle*. What's the real reason you don't want to write a profile of Jonathan Cain?" Maria demanded.

Elizabeth closed her eyes and sighed wearily. "That guy gives me the creeps."

"He does?" Maria replied, surprised that she and Elizabeth felt the same way about him.

An angry spark flashed in Elizabeth's eyes. "I think he's a rude, egotistic jerk," she declared emphatically. "The first time I saw him, he nearly knocked me down, trying to push his way through the hall. Then he shoved Peggy Abbot into a wall and stepped on her history project." Elizabeth's eyes narrowed. "But it's much more than that. I can't really explain it."

Maria nodded thoughtfully. "I think I know what you mean. I get an eerie feeling around him too. And his eyes . . ." She shuddered, remembering a time the week before when Jonathan had looked right at her in the hall between classes.

"And the way people are throwing themselves at him," Elizabeth said. "I think he's a big fake, and it's gross how everyone is trying to copy him."

Maria raised her eyebrows. "Have you seen Enid yet?"

Elizabeth rolled her eyes. "Yeah, I saw her new look, but I haven't had a chance to talk to her."

"I ran into her at the mall last Friday," Maria said. "I wasn't going to tell you, but—"

Elizabeth looked at her curiously. "Why, what happened?"

Maria shrugged, remembering her hurt feelings. "Enid had just come out of the salon." She continued with the story of her encounter with Enid. "She gave me the brush-off in no uncertain terms."

Elizabeth frowned. "That doesn't sound like Enid at all."

"I know," Maria replied. "I think she's feeling threatened because of my friendship with you. Remember how badly Nicole treated you at camp because you and I were friends?"

Elizabeth shook her head. "I think it's much more than that, Maria. I'm positive that something terrible is going on at Sweet Valley High."

"Like what?" Maria asked.

"I don't know," Elizabeth replied in a shaky voice. "But I'm so afraid that my friends are going to be pulled down with it."

Chapter 9

At lunch the following day, Elizabeth headed straight for Enid's table, determined to talk some sense into her friend. She'd tried calling several times the night before, but each time Mrs. Rollins had told her Enid couldn't come to the phone.

Elizabeth's eyes narrowed as she studied the change in her friend's appearance. Enid's lovely curly reddish brown hair had been replaced with a straight black mop, and the healthy glow of her complexion had been covered with a sickly pale cosmetic foundation.

Elizabeth thought Enid looked as though she'd been vandalized, defaced like the side of an old building or a billboard on the highway. Her eyes were heavily circled with black eyeliner and fringed with thick, gooey lashes that looked like spider legs. Her blackish red lipstick made her lips seem as if they were caked with dried blood.

"Why didn't you call me back last night?" Elizabeth asked as she plunked her tray down across from Enid.

Enid looked at her with a bland expression. "Oh, hi, Elizabeth. Nice to see you too."

Elizabeth ripped off the top of her yogurt carton. "I waited up past midnight."

Enid tucked a lock of her new jet black hair behind her ears, revealing a pair of pewter skull-and-crossbones earrings with tiny red stones in the eye sockets. "Sorry. My mom didn't tell me your call was urgent."

"It wasn't exactly urgent," Elizabeth said, forcing the harshness out of her voice. She slowly stirred her yogurt, choosing her words thoughtfully. It wouldn't help matters to antagonize Enid. "I'm worried about you," Elizabeth said finally.

Enid shrugged. "Don't be," she replied. "I've never been better."

"That's what you say, but—" Elizabeth lost her train of thought, distracted by the sight of Enid's black, daggerlike fingernails as she picked up a potato chip and brought it up to her blood red lips.

"What are you staring at?" Enid demanded, glaring across the table. The eyeliner had seeped into her eyes, creating a black watery film along her bottom eyelids, pooling in the corners.

Elizabeth shuddered. "Enid, this obsession of yours is spinning out of control."

"What obsession?" she asked. "Does it bother you that I like a guy you don't approve of? Or is it that I've decided to change a few things about myself without your permission?"

"A *few* things? Look at you, Enid," Elizabeth urged. "I hardly recognize you anymore."

"That's perfectly understandable," Enid snapped. "You haven't seen me in ages. Ever since Maria came back to Sweet Valley, you've been totally ignoring me."

Elizabeth reeled back, as if she'd been stung. "That's not fair," she countered. "You and I are best friends, Enid. We've been through a lot together. You know how much I care what happens to you." Elizabeth took a deep breath and added softly, "I'd like to think that you'd confront me if our situations were reversed."

Enid stood up, grabbing her tray. "Save it for your new best friend—Maria Slater. I'm not interested," Enid said hotly. With that, she began to march off.

"Don't walk away, Enid!" Elizabeth called after

her. But Enid kept on going, her back straight and her shoulders rigid. Elizabeth felt a knot of cold fear in her gut. *Enid is headed for trouble,* she thought. *And there's nothing I can do about it.*

Enid smiled with satisfaction as she stormed off, leaving Elizabeth with her mouth agape. *Who needs a control freak for a best friend, anyway?* Enid asked herself. She was sick of trying to be what everyone else wanted her to be, to fit a mold that no longer fit. Falling in love had completely changed her world.

Enid looked around the crowded, noisy cafeteria and saw a sea of possibilities. *I need new friends,* Enid decided. Lynne Henry, Julie Porter, and Jennifer Mitchell, all of whom had also adopted Jonathan's gothic style of dress, were sitting together at a nearby table. Enid was surprised when Annie Whitman walked over and joined them. Annie usually sat with Jessica Wakefield at the cheerleaders' table.

Curbing her sudden shyness, Enid strode over to the group of girls. "Can I sit here?" she asked hesitantly.

The girls took one look at Enid and welcomed her enthusiastically. *Thank goodness everyone isn't as narrow-minded as Elizabeth,* Enid thought as she sat down.

"I love your nails," Jennifer exclaimed. Her naturally blond hair had been colored a rich, dark sable. "Tell me they're not real! I'd die if I thought perfect nails like that were possible."

Enid laughed. "OK, they're not real. I had them done at the mall."

Annie nodded. "A professional job, that's the only way to go. They're absolutely stunning."

"Thanks," Enid replied, smiling brightly.

"Your eyes are divine," Julie declared.

"They really are," Lynne agreed. "I wish I could put on eyeliner that evenly. Ever since I ditched my glasses for contact lenses, I've really noticed how important eye makeup is."

Enid shrugged modestly. "It's easy. I could show you how."

The girls thanked her exuberantly and immediately began making plans to get together after school for a makeup lesson. *We'll be a genuine cult soon,* Enid thought with a wry grin.

Enid enjoyed looking glamorous and making new friends, but she hadn't forgotten the reason for the changes in her life—Jonathan Cain. She walked out to the parking lot after the last bell on Wednesday, feeling overwhelmed with frustration. She was tired of watching Jonathan from afar, but she hadn't had the guts to talk to him yet. Once he noticed her, Enid was sure he'd fall in love with her completely. *But when?* she wondered impatiently.

She'd driven to school in her mother's blue hatchback that morning. *Jonathan, can't you feel how much I love you?* she thought as she unlocked the doors and tossed her things in the backseat. She slipped behind the wheel and sat for several minutes, watching the stream of students leaving the building, waiting to catch a glimpse of Jonathan.

When she saw him, her heart began to pound. He moved with a powerful stride. Mesmerized, Enid studied him as he walked across the parking lot to his motorcycle. He reminded her of a panther, strong and fierce, but sleek and graceful.

"He's so beautiful," Enid whispered reverently as he kick-started the motorcycle with a determined thrust. "I can't wait any longer," she said with a whimper. She started her mother's car. As the motorcycle roared out of the parking lot, Enid impulsively decided to follow him home.

She stayed a few car lengths behind Jonathan's Harley as he drove through the downtown area of Sweet Valley. She nearly lost him at the busy intersection in front of the courthouse, but she caught up with him at the traffic light on the next block. At one point she ran a stop sign to keep up with the motorcycle, and she nearly collided with an oncoming van. Unfazed, Enid pressed on, determined not to give up the chase. She felt like a wild animal, following the scent of her prey.

They finally arrived at a crumbling mansion in a deserted area on the outskirts of Sweet Valley. The gray paint was chipped and peeling, the front porch looked ready to fall off, and the yard was overgrown with tall weeds. "Where are we?" she whispered to herself.

Enid parked her car some distance away and watched Jonathan enter the forlorn-looking house. A pair of tattered lace curtains hung in the front picture window. Tarnished brass digits, forming the number 225, hung crookedly on a post near the front walk.

"I guess this is home sweet home," she said, surprised. She had imagined a very different sort of house for Jonathan—an elegant, modern design with lots of glass. But if this was where he lived, then she would learn to love the place, ratty old curtains and all.

Enid waited a few minutes, her heart banging so hard she was afraid it might burst through her rib cage. *I can't believe I'm doing this!* she thought. Finally she gathered up her courage and got out of the car.

She picked her steps carefully as she climbed

the broken steps of the front porch and leaned heavily on the doorbell. *I'm shamelessly chasing Jonathan,* she admitted silently. She also knew she couldn't help herself. She had never wanted a guy so much in her life.

Minutes passed as she waited, her whole body trembling with anxiety. To distract herself, she studied the ornate brass door knocker. It was designed in the shape of a grotesque head, with the knocker attached to the monster's nose.

Enid rang the doorbell again. Still no one answered. *It probably doesn't work,* she told herself. She reached for the door knocker and rapped it against the base several times. "I guess you're not just a pretty face around here," Enid whispered at the gruesome design, trying to lighten her mood.

After she'd waited several more minutes, Enid pressed her ear against the door, but there wasn't any sound coming from inside the house. Growing impatient, she banged on the door with her fists. *I know you're home, Jonathan,* she thought, glaring at the door knocker as if it were purposely keeping her away from her soul mate.

Enid left the front door and walked around the house, peering into windows. To her surprise, the inside looked as run-down and abandoned as the outside. Most of the rooms were empty, the floors covered with stained, frayed carpets. One room had a few scattered pieces of furniture—a green couch with torn upholstery, a broken chair, and a large table covered with a dirty sheet of plastic.

With a growing feeling of urgency, Enid searched for any signs of life inside the old house. Through a back window, she could see into what ought to have been a kitchen. But the only appliance was an antique stove—and it was tipped over on its side in the middle of the floor.

No refrigerator, no table . . . something's not right here, Enid realized uneasily. She looked at the stove again, noticing that the bottom was worn through with rust. "I don't think anyone lives in this house," she whispered. Suddenly a large brown rat scurried across the scarred floor. Enid gasped and jumped back from the window.

Spooked and disgusted, she ran back to her car, hopped in, and locked the door. Her shoulders rose and fell as she sucked in huge gulps of air. *Jonathan can't be in that house,* Enid decided as she pulled her keys out of her pocket, her hands shaking. She tried to convince herself that she'd only imagined him going in there.

Enid started the engine and took off, kicking up a spray of gravel. *Maybe I really am going crazy!* she thought. *Enough is enough. Even*

Jonathan isn't worth giving up my sanity. This silly crush business is over, she promised herself.

Without a backward glance, she drove away, anxious to put distance between herself and the creepy mansion.

"Not this, not this . . . ," Jessica grumbled under her breath as she flipped through a rack of dresses in Bibi's on Thursday afternoon. She had come to the Valley Mall straight from school, hoping to find an outfit that would make Jonathan notice her. So far he'd treated her as if she were invisible. But Jessica was sure she could change all that with just the right dress.

"What about this one, Jess?" Lila asked as she held up a cream-colored angora sweaterdress.

"Totally wrong," Jessica snapped.

"What are you talking about?" Lila argued. "It's gorgeous."

"And it would be perfect if I were trying to steal Todd away from Elizabeth," Jessica said with a dramatic shudder. "I'm looking for a dress that will knock Jonathan's socks off, not make him drowsy."

Lila stood before the store's full-length mirror. "I don't know," she insisted, holding the dress under her chin. "I like it. It's exactly the sort of elegant, classic style that a guy with refined tastes would go for."

Jessica snorted. "Meaning Bo?"

"Exactly," Lila replied.

Jessica came up behind Lila and pretended to study the dress thoughtfully. "You're absolutely right, Lila. Bo would look darling in that. Why not have them box it up and ship it to him express?"

Lila stuck out her tongue at Jessica and replaced the dress on the rack. "Don't you think you're going a bit nuts over this guy?" she asked. "I mean, even for *you*."

Jessica sighed, her lips curving in a dreamy smile. "Jonathan is worth it."

Lila wrinkled her nose. "He's a greaser, and a weird one at that. I don't know what you see in him, Jessica. He gives me the creeps."

Jessica ignored the commentary and resumed flipping through the dresses, concentrating on her mission. Bibi's was one of the most expensive boutiques in the mall and one of Jessica's favorite places to shop. But that day it seemed as if the entire store was filled with boring clothes in bland colors.

Suddenly Jessica looked up and saw it: the perfect weapon. It was hanging right out in the open on a wall display. The short red silk dress was beautiful and drop-dead sexy.

A soft-spoken salesclerk asked Jessica if she wanted to try on the dress. "It's the only one we have in stock," the woman said. "I believe it's a size six."

Jessica smiled brightly. "My size. This must be my lucky day," she declared.

In the fitting room, Jessica shimmied into the red dress and stepped in front of the full-length mirror. Turning from side to side, she admired her reflection. The dress was absolutely incredible. *Jonathan won't be able to ignore me when he sees me wearing this,* she thought confidently.

Jessica stepped out of the fitting room to model the dress for Lila. "Isn't it fabulous?"

Lila shrugged. "It's OK, but I still prefer the angora."

Jessica rolled her eyes, then turned to the sales-clerk, who hovered nearby. "I'll take it," Jessica said, handing over her mother's credit card, which she'd "forgotten" to give back after having used it to buy gas for the Jeep a few days earlier.

Feeling pleased, Jessica headed back toward the fitting room. But as she glanced out the store's back window, she saw Jonathan's motorcycle in the parking lot. "Talk about luck," Jessica said, squeal-ing with delight.

Still wearing the red dress, she took off running

for the exit. "Lila, get the credit card and my things from the fitting room," she called over her shoulder.

What am I doing here, surrounded by people? Have I gone mad? Jonathan asked himself as he walked across the parking lot, ignoring the curious looks aimed in his direction.

He hopped on his motorcycle and looked around, noticing how some people averted their eyes when he stared back at them. Others held his gaze, desiring what they didn't understand.

Jonathan closed his eyes and groaned. *I should never have come here,* he chided himself. It was his aching loneliness that had enticed him to this place, causing him to take such a foolish risk.

When will I ever learn? he wondered. Watching people made his pain stronger, his need sharper. Nothing would ever change that fact.

As Jonathan bent over to retie his bootlace, he felt someone jump on the back of his motorcycle. Jonathan froze, his fists clenched. A groan of frustration rattled through his mind. Even without looking, he knew that his passenger was Jessica Wakefield.

Jonathan didn't have to turn around to see her lovely face, her silky blond hair, her bright smile—the image of her beauty was burned into his mind's eye. But he had promised himself that wouldn't get involved with her.

Tell her to go, he ordered himself.

Jessica's long, graceful arms slipped around his waist. Shaken, Jonathan moaned. *Get rid of her now—before it's too late,* the reasonable voice in his head commanded urgently.

Jonathan turned and faced her. "What do you think you're doing?" he demanded. He looked into her eyes and felt as though he were drowning in their blue-green depths.

Jessica raised her eyebrows, looking at him with mock innocence. "I don't know, Jonathan. But maybe if you and I put our heads together, we can figure that one out. Let's see—I don't think I'm baking a cake; I'm definitely not eating a pizza . . ."

Jonathan's lips twitched, and he felt his resolve slipping. Jessica was smiling at him with her whole face, not just her mouth. Her skin glowed with healthy radiance; she was so *alive,* filling him with sensations he'd all but forgotten. He knew he should order her off the bike, but somehow the words refused to be spoken.

OK, just this once, Jonathan bargained with himself. He would give in to this small temptation for now, knowing he would pay—in torturous anguish—for days to come.

Jonathan started the motorcycle. Jessica responded with a delighted cheer and tightened her hold around his waist. He inhaled sharply, his mind swimming.

Questioning his sanity, Jonathan roared out of the parking lot with Jessica at his back, clinging tightly to him.

Chapter 10

The beautiful sights of Sweet Valley seemed to flicker by in a colorful blur as the motorcycle picked up speed. Jessica pressed her cheek against the soft black leather of Jonathan's jacket, her heart brimming with joy. She noticed that the price tag was still attached to her new red dress, flying like a tiny kite from the edge of her sleeve. Jessica threw her head back and laughed, but the sound was swallowed up by the roar of the Harley's engine.

They headed through town, and then Jonathan cut a sharp turn onto the Valley Crest Highway. The bike swerved for an instant, and Jessica gasped, half convinced they were going to topple over and slam into the blacktop. Elizabeth had nearly died in a motorcycle accident some time ago, and the frightening memory sent a chill through Jessica.

But Jonathan quickly regained his balance and deftly steadied the motorcycle. Once again they were racing ahead, cutting a path through the strong ocean breeze. Jessica tightened her arms around Jonathan.

The sun was setting, painting the sky with streaks of purple and red. The Valley Crest Highway was lined with Douglas fir trees that cast long shadows across the road. The wind whipped through Jessica's long blond hair and took her breath away.

She felt an incredible sensation of freedom, as if she and Jonathan were soaring over the ground and might take off for the clouds any second. Being with him was all she had hoped for—and more.

It occurred to Jessica that she was breaking her parents' strict rule against motorcycles. Years ago, one of her cousins had died in a motorcycle accident. And Elizabeth's near-fatal crash had completely convinced her parents that their no-motorcycle rule was well founded.

Jessica pushed the thought away as if it were a pesky little mosquito. She considered it terribly unfair for her to suffer the punishment for her sister's mishap. And besides, when Elizabeth had gotten hurt, Todd had been driving the motorcycle.

There was no comparison in Jessica's mind.

Jonathan has more skill and experience than bor-ing-as-toast Todd Wilkins could wish for in a million years, she reasoned.

After following the scenic highway for some time, Jonathan headed back into town. Jessica hated for the ride to end, but she was sure that this was just the beginning of a long, fabulous romance. She thought of all the wonderful places they could go together on the Harley: Secca Lake . . . Las Palmas Canyon . . .

Jessica had expected Jonathan to ask for directions to her house, but he drove straight to Calico Drive and pulled into the driveway of her family's split-level home without even asking for her address. She hopped off the bike, tingling all over from the glorious ride. She was also surprised—and delighted—that Jonathan knew where she lived. *I guess he hasn't been totally ignoring me,* she realized, smoothing her hands over the now wrinkled red dress.

Jessica stood next to the bike expectantly, positive that Jonathan was about to ask her out. *I love this moment—when the chase is over and two people finally become an official couple,* she thought. "Well, that was some ride," she said, grinning—and waiting.

Jonathan said nothing at first as he tipped his head back and gazed at the darkening sky, as if he were thinking of the right words for a very important moment. Jessica smiled tenderly. *Don't be shy,* she thought, assuming it was the reason for his hesitation.

But when he looked at her, his eyes were hard and cold. "Don't you ever pull a stunt like that again!" he warned her.

Jessica stared at him, stunned.

"You were lucky this time," he remarked gruffly. "But next time, Jessica, I won't be such a gentleman." With that, he took off, the motorcycle roaring down the street.

Jessica watched him go, her mind whirling and her heart pounding. *How could he say such horrible things to me?* she wondered. A small part of her wanted to crumple to the ground, to curl up into a tight ball and cry.

Jessica mentally kicked that whiny part of herself into shape. *It's not over yet!* she thought with determination. When she was at Camp Echo Mountain, Paul also had claimed that he didn't want to have anything to do with her. But Jessica had worn through his defenses—and she'd do the same with Jonathan. And she wouldn't take no for an answer.

Jessica took a deep breath of the fresh night air. She remembered the feel of his black leather jacket against her cheek and the wind in her hair.

Play it cool if you want to, Jonathan Cain, but you know the truth as well as I do, she thought. *We belong together.*

Swinging her arms and smiling, Jessica strolled to the front door. Her spirits were soaring again as she walked inside the house.

Elizabeth was waiting in the doorway, disapproval written all over her face. "What do you think you're doing, Jess?" she demanded. "You know Mom and Dad's rule about motorcycles."

Jessica shrugged, too happy to let her sister's bossy attitude dampen her excitement. "Oops, I goofed."

Elizabeth's eyes narrowed. "And where did you get that dress?"

"And I shopped too." Jessica smiled and headed toward the kitchen. "All in all, it's been a busy day," she said over her shoulder.

"Don't walk away!" Elizabeth protested, raising her voice.

Jessica chuckled. "I have to feed Jasmine and Prince Albert, but you're welcome to tag along and lecture me in the kitchen."

Elizabeth stormed after her. "This isn't funny, Jessica."

"But this is," Jessica said as she stood in the kitchen doorway, watching the kitten and the golden Labrador. Jasmine was stalking Prince Albert's wagging tail. When she suddenly caught it, Prince Albert whirled around and glared at her. Then he licked her squarely on the face. Jasmine scurried across the room and cowered under the butcher-block table.

Jessica laughed. "Aren't they cute?" She opened the bottom cupboard and took out the boxes of dry cat and dog food. "I have a feeling we have the start of a true friendship here," she declared.

Elizabeth was glowering at her. "You weren't even wearing a helmet! Don't you know how dangerous that is? A head injury can leave you paralyzed for life. And that's only if you survive!"

Jessica scooped out bowls of pet food and refilled the water dishes, blocking out her twin's dire warning about the dangers of motorcycles.

"And on top of all that, accepting a ride with someone like Jonathan Cain!" Elizabeth said dramatically.

Jessica washed her hands and grabbed a dish towel. "What are you talking about?" she countered, drying her hands. "Jonathan is totally hot! He's smart and gorgeous. And his bike is equally hot."

"Oh, please, not you too," Elizabeth groaned. "The way people are throwing themselves at that creepy misfit is disgusting."

Jessica threw the dish towel at her sister. "That's

144

enough, Liz. First of all, Jonathan is not a creepy misfit. He's the most exciting guy I've ever met, and he's the best thing to happen to Sweet Valley High in ages. And second, how *dare* you lump me in with those pathetic creatures who are 'throwing themselves' at him? It's not like that at all between us. I *know* that Jonathan is the guy for me, and I'm positive that he feels the same way about me."

Elizabeth shook her head. "He's a big fake."

"And how do you know so much about him?" Jessica objected.

"I just do, that's all," Elizabeth answered.

"He's been in Sweet Valley for less than two weeks and already you're an expert on him?" Jessica asked pointedly.

Elizabeth picked up the dish towel Jessica had thrown and began folding it. "Last Monday morning he nearly knocked me over in the hall as I was walking to my locker. I mean, he just pushed me out of his way. And he didn't apologize or anything."

Jessica raised her eyebrows with mock amazement. "The guy should be shot," she declared sarcastically. "Imagine! He bumped into a student in a crowded hallway and *nearly* knocked her down."

"It was more than that," Elizabeth protested. "He bumped into Peggy Abbot, and she fell to the floor. And he ruined her history project too."

Jessica folded her arms and glared at her twin.

"Peggy Abbot? Are we talking about the cute soph-omore who tried to steal Todd away from you a while back?"

Elizabeth caught her bottom lip between her teeth and nodded. "I don't see what difference that makes. It still wasn't right for Jonathan to push her so hard and step on her papier-mâché castle."

Jessica laughed. "Maybe not, but I for one would've loved to have seen it."

Elizabeth threw the folded dish towel at her. "That's terrible!"

Jessica caught it in one hand. "Lighten up, Elizabeth. OK, so Jonathan was hurrying to class and might've acted rude. That doesn't mean he's a horrible person. Maybe he had something impor-tant on his mind—maybe he was worried about someone in his family."

Elizabeth raised her chin a notch. "Jonathan Cain is bad news. I have a strong feeling about this, Jessica, and I'm worried about you. Stay away from him."

Jessica batted her eyelashes. "Thanks for the advice, Liz, but considering the mess you've made of your love life, I don't think you're in a position to tell me how to behave with guys."

Elizabeth's face turned bright red. She opened her mouth, then closed it again.

It was a small but satisfying victory, and Jessica

smiled triumphantly. *Guess I've made my point,* she thought.

Hunger. The empty, gnawing ache is back. . . .

In the dark hours before dawn, a young man roamed the night, pushed onward by his body's sharp craving. He skulked along a narrow road for miles, ducking away from the piercing lights of passing cars. The hateful, dreaded word seemed to echo in his ears: *hunger* . . .

Clinging to the shadows, he entered the woods near Miller's Point. A sudden blast of music sounded in the distance. His gaze probed the blackness, searching out the source of the noise. He saw a car parked farther up the hill. He also heard clearly the voices inside the car—jovial conversation and bubbling laughter, taunting him, whetting his hunger.

His heart pounded eagerly. Before he realized it was happening, his feet began rushing toward the car. Steadily he climbed higher and higher. *Hunger.* The thought propelled him faster and faster.

Suddenly he was there. The car—his goal—was just within his reach. He crept closer. His hands tingled and his mouth watered in anticipation.

No! his mind screamed. He stopped in his tracks, trembling. He pressed his hands against the sides of his head and moaned, as if the conflict in his brain were an actual battle being fought with guns and knives.

With sheer willpower pushing him on, he staggered, then ran in the opposite direction. His hunger flared, but he kept going, putting distance between him and the car's temptation.

He was near the bottom of the hill when a small animal scurried across his path. The hunter's keen skill was sharpened by his fierce need. He caught the helpless squirrel with his bare hands and sank down to the ground with the squirming animal.

Minutes later, he leaned back against a tree and closed his eyes. An unpleasantly bitter taste lingered on his tongue, but he was relieved that he'd managed not to drink from a human this time. There were other night animals in the woods; he could hear them scampering through the underbrush and climbing in the trees. *Perhaps this might be enough,* he thought hopefully.

But then a vision of long blond hair swam before his eyes. His terrible hunger returned, tearing through his heart with agony.

Jessica could see her diamond earring sparkling just out of her reach as she stepped through knee-deep garbage. "Help me get it, Lila," *she yelled.*

But Lila wasn't there. Jessica was alone, and there was something terrible hiding under the garbage. She couldn't remember what it was, but she knew she would find it soon.

A clump of long blond hair wrapped itself like a snake around her ankle. Her foot struck something solid. Then, with her heart slamming against her rib cage, she looked down at the dead body.

It was her own.

Jessica woke up, startled. Her body felt frozen even though she was drenched in sweat. For a few seconds she lay perfectly still, too afraid to move. Her heart was pounding so hard, she felt as if it were shaking the whole bed.

It was a nightmare, she realized. Only a dream. She took in deep gulps of air and exhaled loudly. As she calmed down a bit Jessica became aware of her surroundings. It was the middle of the night, she was in her own room, and Jasmine was nearby, yowling crazily.

Jessica sat up and glanced around in the darkness. The digital display of the clock radio on her bedside table read 3:00 A.M. The numbers cast a red glow over her room. She could see Jasmine standing next to the window, her paws clawing at the wall as if she were trying to climb to the windowsill. A cat that howls at the moon? Jessica thought wryly.

She yawned and rubbed her eyes, trying to shake off the last of the cold tremors left over from her nightmare. Again she reminded herself it had been a dream, and she climbed out of bed.

As usual, Jessica's carpet was strewn from wall to wall with discarded clothes, CDs, shoes, and magazines. She stepped gingerly through the piles of debris as she made her way across the room.

"What's the matter?" she whispered as she bent down and scooped up the kitten. "Did you have a bad dream too, Jasmine?"

The kitten answered with a plaintive cry and pushed her head in the crook of Jessica's neck. "Hey, it's OK," Jessica cooed. "Nothing will hurt you in here."

She noticed the window was open a crack. As she leaned over to close it, Jessica saw something sparkle on the windowsill. "How strange," she whispered, bending over to take a better look. "My diamond earring!" she cried. Jasmine began to howl and claw at Jessica's shoulders.

Jessica yelped in pain and grabbed the kitten's paws. Holding Jasmine at arm's length, Jessica looked into the kitten's yellow eyes. "Take it easy," she said in a warning tone. Then she snuggled Jasmine to her chest, keeping a tight hold on the kitten's paws.

Jessica picked up the earring carefully. Ignoring

her cat's hissing and attempts to get free, she held the earring in her open palm and studied it. The diamond appeared red in the clock radio's light. *Has it been there the whole time—or did someone just put it there?* she wondered.

As Jessica glanced through the window at the dark, empty street below, she shivered, and a knot of fear clenched in her stomach.

Chapter 11

Jessica followed behind Lila as they walked out of Mr. Frankel's classroom after math on Friday afternoon. ". . . and then Bo called me back," Lila continued over her shoulder, "and we both watched the same video—alone, but together."

"Sounds wild," Jessica mumbled sarcastically.

Lila stopped at the door of the girls' room. "It was a great movie," she insisted.

Jessica gave her a little shove. The last-period bell would be ringing in less than two minutes. "Hurry up, Lila. I don't want to be late for class."

Lila flashed her a coy smile and pushed the door open. Jessica headed straight for the mirrors and fumbled through her bag for her hairbrush. She considered herself lucky to have such shiny, healthy-looking blond hair. Of course, her twin's hair was equally lovely. But unlike Elizabeth, who always pinned her hair back with hair clips or tied it in a braid or ponytail, Jessica thought hers looked best worn down, hanging freely. She assumed most guys preferred it that way too. *But Jonathan isn't like most guys,* she reminded herself.

Jessica piled her hair on her head and held it with one hand. "Maybe I should have worn my hair up today," she said, turning her face from side to side as she studied her reflection.

Lila gasped. "You found your earring! Where was it?"

Remembering, Jessica's smile faded. She could easily picture the earring on her windowsill and hear Jasmine's howling. Jessica let go of her hair and watched it tumble down over her shoulders. "It was in my room," she answered quickly.

"How do you suppose it got there?" Lila asked incredulously.

"Maybe when it fell out of my ear, it got stuck in my sweater or jacket." *I wish I believed that,* Jessica thought as she pulled out a tube of lipstick.

"That was lucky," Lila remarked.

Jessica recalled the creepy nightmare she'd had right before she'd found the earring. Her hand trembled slightly, causing her to slip up as she applied her lipstick. Grumbling, she grabbed a paper towel.

"The film was a French romance with a mystery subplot, set in Monte Carlo," Lila explained, brushing her hair next to Jessica. "*Le Dessous des Cartes*. That means 'the underside of the cards.' I was surprised the Video Stop even had it. It was marvelous—so surreal, and yet universal. The love story was so gripping, it nearly made me cry. Bo says I have a sensitive soul."

Jessica pressed her lips together as she studied her reflection with a critical eye. "What do you think of this shade?" she asked Lila.

"Romance is so marvelous," Lila declared.

Jessica smiled. "It's called Sweet Summer Kiss."

Lila frowned. "What is?"

"My lipstick." Jessica slipped the tube into her bag and began brushing her hair.

"I was talking about my date last night with Bo," Lila said in a huffy tone.

Jessica raised her eyebrows. "I thought Bo was in Washington, D.C."

Lila puffed out her cheeks and exhaled. "That's the whole point, Jessica. Bo and I rented the same video and then talked on the phone as we watched it. I swear, since you've started chasing after Jonathan Cain, you've turned into a complete airhead."

Jessica giggled. "I'm sorry, but I don't consider watching videos with a guy who's hundreds of miles away a *date*." She smiled dreamily. "A date is when he takes you on a motorcycle ride and you've got your arms wrapped around him. . . ."

"I suppose it does take a certain level of sophistication to appreciate foreign culture," Lila boasted in a haughty tone. "It's not fair for me to expect you to understand these things,"

Jessica dropped her hairbrush into her bag. "*Au contraire,*" she responded with a saucy grin. "That's French for 'you don't know what you're talking about,'" she added.

Lila snorted. "Actually, it means 'on the contrary.'"

"Same thing," Jessica said. "And for your information, I love French. It's my favorite subject." She gave herself another once-over inspection and flung her bag over her shoulder. "Come on. I don't want to be late for class."

Jonathan was already there when Jessica entered the classroom. She took the seat next to his and flashed him a bright smile. As usual, he ignored her.

I love a challenge, she thought, completely undaunted by his attitude. She was sure that he was trying to cover up his feelings because he couldn't face his attraction to her. Jessica picked up her pen and opened her notebook. She thought for a moment, then began to write. *Dear Jonathan: Thanks for yesterday.*

The bell rang, and Ms. Dalton began the class. Jessica glanced at Jonathan and smiled. He was staring straight ahead, pretending to be enthralled with Ms. Dalton's review of singular and plural noun endings. His long black hair was tousled a bit, as if it had been blown by the wind. Jessica had a strong urge to run her fingers through it.

She sighed deeply and turned back to the page in her notebook. *I know you had fun too,* she wrote. *When are you going to take me for another ride on your motorcycle?* She signed it *Love, Jessica.* When Ms. Dalton's back was turned, Jessica slipped the note onto Jonathan's desk.

Jonathan slapped his hand on the folded sheet of paper, as if he were swatting a fly. The wooden, silver, and onyx ring on his middle finger made a dull, hollow sound against the desktop. Jessica held her breath, waiting.

After a few long moments Jonathan closed his hand, crumpling the paper in his fist without having read it. Then he threw it on the floor as if it were nothing more than a piece of garbage. Jessica's jaw dropped as she stared in him in disbelief.

Ms. Dalton called on Jonathan to translate something from the board. He answered correctly, his voice smooth and firm. Apparently throwing away Jessica's note hadn't bothered him in the least.

Jessica looked at the wad of white paper on the floor. Tears stung in her eyes, and her heart felt as if it too, had been crumpled and tossed aside. *Is he really rejecting me?* she wondered. *For real?*

Elizabeth stared at the blank computer screen in the *Oracle* office. *Why can't I think?* she asked herself. She'd stayed after school to work on her article about child actors, but so far she hadn't written even one sentence.

The cursor kept blinking at her as if it were a foot tapping impatiently. Across the room, Allen and Olivia were going over page proofs. Although they kept their voices low, the slightest sound broke Elizabeth's concentration.

Who am I kidding? she asked herself. She knew she couldn't blame her lack of concentration on anyone but herself. Her mind was whirling madly on its own, refusing to obey Elizabeth's orders.

Ever since she'd found the Camp Echo Mountain paddle in her locker on Monday morning, Elizabeth hadn't been able to think clearly about anything. She expected Joey to show up again, and not knowing when was driving her crazy. But she didn't think it would be wise to call him. She didn't want him to get the wrong idea—to think that she was interested in seeing him again. *Even though I am* . . . Elizabeth shook her head, pushing away that thought. Her relationship with Todd was too important for her to take any more foolish risks.

But what if Joey comes here again today? she wondered, her heart picking up speed.

"Hey, Elizabeth, it's after four o'clock—I think the weekend officially started ten minutes ago," Allen announced.

Elizabeth looked up and saw that he and Olivia were leaving. "I'm going to stay and finish my article," she responded.

When she was alone, Elizabeth became aware of the empty silence in the school building, and an eerie feeling came over her. *That's enough. Stop procrastinating and get to work this instant!* she ordered herself.

She forced everything but the subject of child actors out of her mind and scanned her hand-written notes, adding a few more ideas as they occurred to her. Maria had mentioned that she'd lost a movie role at the age of eleven because the project had been canceled. Elizabeth made a note to ask Maria about the disappointments child actors faced.

Suddenly Elizabeth froze, startled by a noise coming from the hallway. A door had slammed, and now footsteps were heading her way. Her heart skipped a beat. The pencil she'd been using fell to the floor. *Joey*, she thought excitedly. *He's come back*. She held her breath as she watched the door expectantly. The footsteps stopped. Elizabeth felt as if she were ready to explode with anticipation. An image of Joey's beautiful green eyes flashed through her mind. *What will I say to him?* she wondered.

But it was Jonathan Cain who appeared at the door. Elizabeth gasped, recoiling in horror. She was more than disappointed. The sight of his pale face and feverish blue eyes made her skin crawl. She felt as if she'd lifted the lid off a surprise gift and found a snake nestled in the tissue paper.

"I know how much power you have over your sister, Elizabeth," he said, pinning her with his gaze.

Elizabeth gulped. She tried to find her voice, but when she opened her mouth, all that came out was a soft, wheezy squeak.

Jonathan's eyes narrowed slightly. "If you want to protect Jessica, keep her away from me."

Elizabeth wanted to ask him what he meant, but before she could say anything, Jonathan was gone. She jumped up and ran into the hall, but there was no sign of him. Everything was silent. The only sound was her own labored breathing.

Elizabeth went back inside the *Oracle* office. Shivering, she shut the door and leaned against it.

She knew with gut certainty that Jonathan Cain was going to bring disaster to Sweet Valley High.

How can I convince Jessica to stay away from that creep? she wondered desperately.

Jessica sat by herself in a booth at the Dairi Burger, still reeling from Jonathan's cruel rejection. *I should hate him,* she pouted as she dragged a french fry through a puddle of ketchup. *No guy is worth this much trouble.*

But Jessica knew that wasn't true. *Jonathan is worth everything,* she admitted to herself glumly.

The Dairi Burger was deserted, as it had been since the night of the murder, but Jessica had felt drawn to it. She also found it to be the perfect place to wallow in self-pity.

Jessica shredded the paper napkin on her tray. She could still see Jonathan's beautiful long fingers crumpling her note. Even then, she hadn't lost hope. After class, she'd hurried out of the room and hid near the doorway, watching to see if Jonathan would take a peek at her note if he thought she wasn't looking. But he'd stepped on the wad of paper without a glance.

Remembering, a fresh wave of hurt and shame washed over Jessica. *How could he do that to me?* she wondered. *Why can't he just admit that he cares for me?*

A movement on the other side of the restaurant caught her attention. Jessica noticed a dark-haired girl sitting over there by herself. She was wearing the new gothic look that had become popular at Sweet Valley High since Jonathan's arrival. But the thick black circles of eyeliner and the purplish red lipstick couldn't cover up the gloomy look on the girl's face.

Jessica could read that look as easily as if it were written in tall letters on a billboard. *Guy trouble,* she told herself. *It must be an epidemic around here.*

The girl pushed her hair behind her ears and dabbed her eyes with a paper napkin. Jessica frowned. There was something familiar about her. . . .

Oh, my gosh, it's Enid! Jessica realized, amazed. The transformation was incredible. Enid looked almost glamorous. *I guess the magazine ads are true—with the right cosmetics and clothes, even a total nerd has a chance,* Jessica thought.

She wondered who the guy in Enid's life was. Most of the girls who were wearing the gothic style had massive crushes on Jonathan, but Jessica considered Enid too smart to go after someone so obviously out of her league. The poor girl was probably pining over someone who wore thick glasses and whose idea of a hot Saturday night was computer chess and baloney sandwiches.

Still, it might be nice to talk to someone who understands what I'm going through, Jessica thought. She debated whether or not to join Enid. They were the only customers in the Dairi Burger, so it wasn't as if Jessica ran the risk of being seen with her.

What the heck, even Elizabeth's drippy friend is a better ear than no ear at all, Jessica decided as she carried her milkshake and plate of fries over to Enid's booth.

Enid looked up with eyes that were red and puffy.

Jessica set her things down on the table and slid into the booth. "Let me guess—you've just had your heart smashed to bits by some cold, unfeeling jerk," she said.

Enid blinked. "How did you know?"

Jessica shrugged. "Join the club."

"He acts as if he doesn't even know I exist," Enid said.

Jessica popped a french fry into her mouth and nodded as she chewed thoughtfully. "Sounds familiar."

"I wish I could forget him," Enid cried. "But I can't stop thinking about him. He's so gorgeous. I keep seeing his mysterious dark blue eyes in my mind. I know we could have something special together, but . . ." Her voice trailed off, and her eyes filled with tears.

Blue eyes? She couldn't possibly be talking about Jonathan, Jessica thought suspiciously. "Have you known this guy for very long?" she asked, keeping her voice casual.

Enid shook her head. "No, but ever since I first saw him last Monday, I've felt as if I've known him forever."

Jessica realized Enid *was* talking about Jonathan, and her jaw dropped. *She actually believes she has a chance with him!* Jessica thought.

"No one understands how much I love him," Enid continued. "I haven't been able to eat or sleep, and I'm flunking every subject. Elizabeth thinks I'm crazy, and maybe I am. But I know he's the one guy for me."

Jessica nodded slowly. Now she understood why her twin had been so up in arms about Jonathan. Elizabeth was happiest when she was in complete control of her life, and she thought everyone else should try to do the same. She would hate any guy who had caused her best friend's grades to slip. Elizabeth considered good grades to be nearly as important as air, water, and food.

Tears streamed down Enid's face, creating a black watery mess of eye makeup. "I just have to meet him. But nothing seems to work. I even followed him home after school a few days ago."

Jessica raised her eyebrows. "Oh, really?" *Why didn't I think of that?* she wondered.

Enid nodded. "When I got to his house, he wouldn't even answer the door. I chickened out and ran." She began to sob fresh tears.

"Does he live near you?" Jessica asked, trying not to be obvious about pumping for information.

Enid shook her head and sniffed. "He lives way out on the edge of town, on Forrest Lane."

"Forrest Lane is very long. Are you sure you had the right house?" Jessica asked.

"I told you, I followed him," Enid explained. "He pulled into the driveway of number two-twenty-five and walked in the front door."

Jessica made a mental note of the address and slid out of the booth. "This has been great fun, Enid, but I've got to run. Help yourself to the rest of my french fries." Leaving Enid in tears, Jessica rushed out of the Dairi Burger, already planning her new strategy.

She hummed along with the radio as she pulled out of the parking lot. Jessica felt inspired, and she was more determined than ever to catch Jonathan. Enid had given her a whole new direction in which to plan her mission. *It sure helps to talk things over with someone who understands*, Jessica thought, chuckling.

She took her time driving home, taking a detour along the Valley Crest Highway. The sun was setting, as it had been the day before, when she and Jonathan had driven over the same stretch of road. Jessica sighed, remembering how wonderful it had felt to ride with her arms around him and the wind in her hair. *Jonathan and I are going to come back here often,* she vowed.

The western sky was deep orange and a few stars were already out when Jessica arrived home. She hopped out of the Jeep, still thinking about Jonathan. But as she headed up the front walk, she heard Elizabeth's voice in the backyard, calling for Jasmine.

An alarm went off in Jessica's head. She ran inside the house, headed straight through the kitchen, and yanked open the sliding glass door that led to the back patio. "What's going on?" she asked Elizabeth.

Elizabeth looked worried. "Jasmine got out, and I can't find her."

"What?" Jessica stepped outside and glared at her sister. "How could you be so careless, Liz?"

Elizabeth glared back at her. "I didn't do it on purpose. I heard a strange noise outside the house, and when I opened the door to see what it was, Jasmine raced out before I could stop her."

Jessica felt heartbroken as she imagined her

beloved kitten wandering around lost and frightened. "She's so small. What if she can't find her way back? What if she gets hit by a car?"

"Come on, let's split up and search the neighborhood," Elizabeth instructed, giving Jessica a gentle shove. "And after we find her, you can explain why you took the Jeep and left me stranded at school this afternoon."

"My kitten might be in terrible danger," Jessica shot back. "How can you even think about a ride home from school at a time like this?"

Chapter 12

"Jasmine, where are you?" Jessica called desperately. It was dark out now, and she still hadn't found her kitten. She'd knocked on every door on the block, asking her neighbors if they'd seen a white and gray kitten. No one had.

Tears pooled in Jessica's eyes as she headed back toward her house. She was afraid she'd never see her kitten again, but she refused to give up hope. She cupped her hands around her mouth and yelled "Jasmine!" over and over again.

When she was a few houses away from her own, Jessica thought she heard the familiar sound of Jasmine's distinctive meow coming from a short distance away. She stood still and listened. There it was again. Jessica breathed a sigh of relief and took off running.

She saw the kitten in a tree in front of the Beckwiths' house, which was next door to her family's. Jasmine was meowing frantically and clawing at the tree bark, obviously frightened.

Jessica stopped in her tracks. The scene reminded her of the night she'd found the kitten behind the Dairi Burger—the same night she'd found the dead body in the Dumpster. A creepy feeling came over Jessica, sending chills up and down her spine. *Why is Jasmine so upset this time?* she wondered. *Has she seen something horrible again?*

A shadowy figure suddenly stepped out from behind the tree. Jessica's heart plunged. *What if that's the killer and Jasmine recognizes him?* she thought, terrified.

Then the shadow stepped under the streetlight, and his face became clearly visible. It was Jonathan.

Jessica covered her mouth and laughed giddily. *I don't believe it!* she thought. The guy had crushed her heart only a few hours before, and now he was hanging out in her neighbor's front yard. *Men are so illogical,* she told herself.

Keeping to the soft, grassy area of the Beckwiths' lawn, Jessica sneaked up behind Jonathan. Just as she was about to put her hands over his eyes and say "Guess who?" he spun around and faced her.

Jessica grinned openly, but Jonathan stepped back. He seemed frightened. *I knew it,* Jessica thought smugly. *Guys can be so predictable at times.*

"Don't tell me, Jonathan," she said, confronting him directly. "You just *happen* to be in my neighborhood, but you really aren't interested in seeing me, right?"

He didn't react at all. The expression on his face looked like a stone mask.

Jessica was sure it was all a big act to hide his strong feelings for her. She put her hands on her hips and flashed him a teasing smile. "Let me guess—you don't trust me because some silly girl broke your poor heart ages ago. Or maybe you're afraid I'm interested in you for the wrong reasons—because I like your motorcycle or because I want you to help me with my French homework."

Jonathan looked at her, and something flickered in the depths of his blue eyes. Jessica stopped talking, mesmerized by his intense gaze. Above them, Jasmine was going crazy in the tree, howling, hissing, and clawing at the bark.

"Get your cat and go home, Jessica," Jonathan ordered, pronouncing each word carefully. "You don't know who might be out tonight."

Jessica nodded mutely. *How did he know it was my kitten?* she wondered briefly. But he had sounded so authoritative that she obeyed him automatically, without question. She climbed the tree and coaxed Jasmine to come to her. The kitten was shaking.

"It's OK," Jessica cooed, petting her and nuzzling her fur. When Jasmine had calmed down a bit, Jessica climbed down the tree, keeping a firm hold on the cat.

But when she returned to Jonathan's side, the kitten hissed at him. "Hey, settle down," Jessica said softly. "It's all right, sweetie. This is my friend Jonathan." She moved closer to him.

Jasmine tried to claw his face.

Jessica stepped back and snuggled the trembling kitten tightly. "Sorry about that," she remarked to Jonathan. "She gets scared easily."

Jonathan stared at the whimpering kitten. "Take a lesson from your cat. Beware of predators," he warned Jessica. "They come in all shapes and sizes."

"What is that supposed to mean?" she asked.

He looked up and pinned her with his piercing gaze. Jessica swallowed, her heart pounding. For a long time they stood there, staring into each other's eyes. He was so beautiful, Jessica felt dizzy just looking at him.

A lock of his thick, black hair had fallen over his forehead; Jessica longed to reach out and gently push it back with her fingers. His dark red lips were scowling at her; she wanted so badly to kiss him, her knees were shaking.

She glanced at the wooden ring on Jonathan's middle finger. The silver inlay gleamed, and the onyx was pure black, darker than the night. *He's the most mesmerizing guy I've ever known,* she thought.

Just then she heard the sound of her twin's voice calling Jasmine. Jessica blinked, as if she'd been yanked from a wonderful dream. Jonathan stepped back into the shadows. Reluctantly Jessica turned away from him and saw Elizabeth coming down the street, waving a flashlight. "Come out now, Jasmine," Elizabeth called.

"I found her," Jessica answered loudly enough for her sister to hear. Then, lowering her voice to a whisper, she turned back to Jonathan and said, "I have to go, Jonathan. Why don't you call me—" The rest of her words died on her lips. He was gone.

Jessica stared at the spot where he had been standing a second earlier. *It's as if he melted into the darkness,* she mused.

Her whole body was trembling with a mixture of fear and excitement. Jonathan was the most incredible guy she'd ever met. With just a look he could make her feel things she'd never before imagined. Each time he pushed her away, her need for him doubled.

You're going to be mine soon, Jonathan, she promised herself. *I will find a way.*

Elizabeth was furious as she followed her twin into the house. She'd caught a glimpse of the guy Jessica had been talking to, and she didn't like it one bit. "What was *he* doing here?" Elizabeth demanded.

"Who?" Jessica asked with mock innocence as she carried Jasmine into the kitchen and set her down on the floor. "There you go, sweetie. Isn't it great to be home? And look, your dish is full. Won't a big bowl of fishy-tasting crunchy things hit the spot right now?"

Elizabeth crossed her arms and gave her sister an I-mean-business look. "You know who I mean, Jess."

Jessica raised her eyebrows. "He has a name."

"That doesn't answer my question," Elizabeth said impatiently.

Jessica sighed exasperatedly. "Jonathan just happened to be in the neighborhood. And I'm not interested in hearing you say terrible things about the guy I love," she huffed. "How about some fresh water, Jasmine?"

Elizabeth sat down at the table. "I've suspected all along there was something strange about that guy. Now I know it for sure."

Jessica refilled the cat's water dish and set it on the floor. "Would my special kitty also like some milk?"

Elizabeth exhaled loudly. "Quit playing games, Jess."

Jessica turned to her with a stubborn look. "There's nothing you can say that will make me stop caring for Jonathan."

Elizabeth glared at her. "Would you just *listen?*"

Jessica shrugged her shoulder. "Go ahead, I'm listening."

"Jonathan came into the *Oracle* office this afternoon when I was working on my article. He told me to keep you away from him." Elizabeth shuddered at the memory of his blazing eyes staring at her. "It was so eerie."

Jessica raised her fists in victory and cried, "Yes!"

Elizabeth stared at her, speechless. *My sister is completely nuts,* she thought.

"Don't you see what this means?" Jessica said. "Jonathan wants you to keep me away from him because he realizes that he won't be able to resist me for too much longer. I'm almost there!"

Elizabeth gaped at her twin. "You don't get it, do you, Jess? You're going to get yourself in deep trouble if you don't stop chasing him."

Jessica grinned smugly and walked over to the

refrigerator. "Don't worry, I won't have to chase Jonathan much longer," she replied as she studied the contents of the refrigerator.

A flash of alarm went off in Elizabeth's mind. "Jessica, you have to promise me you won't go near Jonathan Cain again," she insisted.

Jessica chuckled. "Are we out of salsa?"

Totally exasperated, Elizabeth slapped her hand against the tabletop and shrieked, "You're not even listening to me, are you?"

"Of course I'm listening," Jessica said, not bothering to lift her head out of the refrigerator. "You want me to stay away from Jonathan even though he's the hottest guy I've ever met and clearly the key to my future happiness."

"I'm not kidding, Jessica," Elizabeth warned. "This is serious."

Jessica giggled. "It would serve him right if I did stay away from him. Maybe it would force him to make a move."

Elizabeth rolled her eyes and groaned. Sometimes Jessica acted as if she didn't have a single brain cell in her skull. "Consider the facts," Elizabeth said, trying to keep her voice sounding calm. "There's a terrible murder in Sweet Valley, and then Jonathan shows up. People start acting weird—"

Jessica whirled around, her eyes wide in a challenging look. "This is all about Enid, isn't it? You think Jonathan is terrible because your best friend has a crush on him and her grades have dropped." She wrinkled her nose. "What are low grades to Enid, anyway? Anything below an A minus?"

Elizabeth sighed wearily. "I didn't know about Enid's grades. I'm concerned about her, yes. But I'd still be worried about you even if Enid weren't acting so strange lately. You have to trust me on this, Jessica. I'm begging you to stay away from Jonathan."

Jessica twisted a lock of her hair around her finger for a few seconds as she thought. Then she looked at Elizabeth and said, "I'll promise to stay away from Jonathan—unless he asks me out. Then the deal is off."

Elizabeth glared at her. Jessica sighed dramatically. "For how long?" she asked.

"Until we know more about him," Elizabeth replied. "A few weeks, maybe a month."

"OK, I promise to stay away from him for a few weeks," Jessica conceded. "There, are you satisfied?"

"I just know Jonathan is a door to disaster," Elizabeth said emphatically.

Jessica raised her chin defiantly. "I just promised to stay away from him, so quit lecturing me. Now let's talk about something really important.

How about a huge bowl of chocolate mint ice cream to celebrate Jasmine's homecoming?"

Elizabeth rolled her eyes, but she walked over to the silverware drawer and took out two spoons and the ice cream scoop. She couldn't understand why Jonathan seemed to have such power over women. She suspected that Jessica had been crossing her fingers when she'd promised to stay away from him. *I'll just have to keep close tabs on Jessica for the next few days,* Elizabeth decided.

Jessica climbed out of the pool on Saturday night and wrapped a towel around her shoulders. "I'm ready for a hot shower now," she said to Elizabeth, who was reading in a lawn chair next to the pool.

Elizabeth looked up from her book and smiled. "Hasn't this been a great day? Just the two of us hanging out around the house."

"It's been loads of fun," Jessica replied, keeping the sarcasm out of her voice. "And I can't wait to watch the videos you've rented."

Elizabeth's eyes narrowed slightly. "Really?"

Jessica ducked her head sheepishly. *Don't overdo it,* she warned herself. Her plan wouldn't work if Elizabeth became the least bit suspicious. "I have to keep up with Lila, you know. She's turning into more of a snob than ever since she's met Bo."

Elizabeth laughed. "I don't know if *The African Queen* and *The Maltese Falcon* can compare to Lila's foreign-film craze, but Humphrey Bogart is fabulous. But mostly I'm glad to be spending time with you, Jessica. We should do this more often."

Jessica winced inwardly at something that came close to a twinge of guilt. She covered it up with a giggle. "Sure, let's make it a regular thing. The Wakefield twins' Saturday night retreat."

Jessica ran up the stairs to her room and sprang into action. Elizabeth had been sticking to her like glue for the past twenty-four hours, but Jessica had come up with a brilliant plan to outsmart her nosy sister.

She rushed into the bathroom that she and Elizabeth shared, which connected their rooms. Jessica locked the doors and hopped into the shower. She would have liked to spend a long time luxuriating under the warm spray, but there was too much to be done in a very short time.

When Jessica stepped out of the shower a few minutes later, she left the water running and padded back to her bedroom. *This is the night my dreams will come true,* she mused. And it had nothing to do with watching Humphrey Bogart videos with her sister. Jessica giggled. In her opinion, *dry, colorless,* and *long-lasting* were words more appropriate for antiperspirants, not movies.

She opened her closet and took out the blue silk dress she'd picked out earlier. Holding it out at arm's length, she looked it over again. It was long, with full-length narrow sleeves and a scooped neckline trimmed with delicate white lace. It was very different from her usual style, but after much consideration, she'd decided it would be perfect for that night.

The sexy red dress she'd bought the week before had worked to capture Jonathan's attention. Jessica smiled as she remembered the price tag still dangling from the red sleeve during their wonderful motorcycle ride.

But that night she needed something that would show off her deeper, more serious side. Jessica wanted to show Jonathan that she had more to offer than superficial beauty and fun times. After all, Jonathan was much more than a black-leather-clad motorcycle rider. She'd seen the dark intensity in his eyes. And her blond, all-American good looks didn't prevent her from being strong and courageous enough to face that part of him. *This dress is perfect,* she decided as she laid it across her rumpled bed.

Moving with lightning speed, Jessica dried her hair and applied her makeup. She'd decided to keep the accessories simple—just a black velvet choker around her neck and her diamond earrings. When she was ready to leave, she glanced in the mirror one last time. Her blue-green eyes sparkled with anticipation. "Tonight, Jonathan," she whispered.

Jessica went into the bathroom and turned off the shower. Then she ducked back into her room and opened the hall door a crack. "Elizabeth, the bathroom is free," she called downstairs. When she heard Elizabeth get into the shower, Jessica bolted from her room. She rushed downstairs and turned on the television to mask the sounds of her escape. But just as she was leaving, Jasmine raced out the door after her.

"No, Jasmine," Jessica whispered harshly. She chased the kitten across the front lawn. "Come back here, naughty kitten!" She finally nabbed her in the driveway.

"You can't come with me this time, Jasmine," Jessica said as she carried her to the door. "I don't need a chaperon." She put the cat back inside and hurried to the Jeep, her heart racing.

I should be with Jonathan tonight, Enid thought as she paced across her bedroom. When she'd first fallen in love with him, her biggest obstacle had been her shyness. She still hadn't man-

181

aged to talk to him, even though she'd practiced in front of her mirror hundreds of times. But now it seemed that everyone who professed to care about her had turned against her when she'd needed them most—her mother, Elizabeth . . .

Enid slapped her fist against her open palm. She'd supported Elizabeth through all sorts of disasters, but now that Enid could use a bit of support, her so-called best friend was too busy with Maria Slater to listen.

Enid's mother had flipped out the day before after receiving a call from Mrs. Green, a busybody guidance counselor with a big mouth. *So my grades are slipping a bit. Big deal!* Enid thought hotly. She was exhausted from having argued with her mother all day. *When did being late with a history report turn into a major crime?* she wondered.

No one seemed to understand the depth of her feelings for Jonathan. If they did, she was sure they'd understand why homework assignments, unit exams, and science labs had become meaningless to her. But because of Mrs. Green's warning, Enid was grounded indefinitely—or, as her mother had put it, until she'd managed to pull her "grades and attitude out of the ditch."

Enid knew the cause of her failing grades was Jonathan, but she couldn't give him up, couldn't stop dreaming about him. Her longing for him was unbearably strong, and it hurt to be away from him. She had promised herself to forget her crush on Jonathan, but it was impossible. *How can I live without my soul mate?* she wondered.

She took a deep breath and stared at herself in the mirror above her dresser. "Why can't Jonathan see how perfect I am for him?" she asked her reflection. *I have to talk to him,* she decided. She didn't want to wait any longer. Waiting wasn't getting her anywhere.

Enid quickly changed into a short black dress and touched up her makeup. Her mother had complained about her new style too, claiming that her daughter had turned into a "freak-show queen."

Enid clenched her teeth, blinking back the sudden tears. She remembered how Elizabeth had looked at her with disgust the last time they'd spoken. *I'm taking the most important step of my life, and my mother and best friend have nothing more to offer than nitpicky fashion advice!* Enid thought. But Jonathan would understand how she felt, she was certain. *We are soul mates, after all,* she reminded herself. She imagined herself curled up in his arms, talking softly, losing herself in his gorgeous blue eyes, kissing his dark, full lips . . .

I have to go, she thought urgently. She pushed her feet into a pair of black boots and grabbed her jacket. Her mother was quietly reading in the living room. Enid slipped past her and rushed out the back door.

She jumped into her mother's car, taking care not to make a sound when she shut the door. Enid's hands were shaking so badly, she could barely manage to stick the key into the ignition. "I'm going to be with Jonathan soon," she whispered, her heart fluttering wildly as she drove out of the driveway and headed toward the lonely old mansion.

Chapter 13

Elizabeth slipped into her oldest, most comfortable pair of faded blue jeans and combed out her damp hair. She was glad that Jessica had suggested a swim after dinner. The exercise and the hot shower afterward had done wonders for Elizabeth's state of mind. She felt relaxed and looked forward to curling up to watch a good movie. Along with the Humphrey Bogart movies, she had also rented an action-adventure video that she thought Jessica would enjoy, and she was planning to surprise her with it.

Elizabeth popped her head out the door. The television had been turned on, presumably by Jessica. "Hey, Jess, why don't you make some popcorn?" Elizabeth called downstairs.

Spending the day with her sister was turning

out to be more fun than Elizabeth had expected. She realized she had been neglecting Jessica lately and was glad for the chance to make it up to her— even though Elizabeth's real motive had been to keep Jessica out of trouble.

Elizabeth ducked back into her room and opened her closet. She made a point of ignoring Joey's canoe paddle, which she'd hidden in the back corner. She had considered displaying it prominently in her room—after all, Camp Echo Mountain had been a learning experience involving more than just her romance with Joey Mason. But until she could look at the paddle and not feel her heart jump to her throat, she decided it would remain tucked away in the back of her closet.

Elizabeth took out a fuzzy gray sweater, equally as comfortable as her jeans, and finished getting dressed. Sitting cross-legged on her chaise longue, she hummed along with the radio as she began weaving her hair into a French braid.

Suddenly the music was interrupted by a news bulletin. "The body of a young woman was found near Secca Lake this evening by an elderly couple."

Elizabeth shuddered as a whisper of terror passed through her. Her hands fell to her lap, abandoning the unfinished braid.

"Police have not yet identified the body—a

Caucasian woman with blond hair, believed to be in her mid- to late teens. The cause of death has been confirmed as exsanguination, the draining of the blood." The announcer's smooth voice seemed strange in light of the ghastly event he described. "There are no suspects at this time, but police believe this case may be connected to the recent murder of Big Mesa High School student Dean Maddingly, whose body was discovered . . ."

Elizabeth's twin radar buzzed. She could always tell when her sister was in trouble. *But Jessica is home with me tonight,* she reminded herself. It didn't seem to make any sense, but Elizabeth couldn't shake the feeling that something was desperately wrong. She jumped up and ran downstairs, suddenly anxious to see her sister and to make sure that she was safe.

The television was blaring, but Jessica wasn't watching it, as Elizabeth had assumed. She turned it off and checked in the kitchen, but found it empty. "Jessica, where are you?" she called.

Elizabeth ran back upstairs and banged on her sister's door. "Jessica, are you there?" There was no answer. Elizabeth peeked inside the room. The place was a disaster, as usual, but Jessica wasn't there. Elizabeth tore through the rest of the house, checking every room. "Jessica, answer me!" she cried.

After she'd searched everywhere, including the laundry room in the basement—even though the idea of Jessica's washing clothes on a Saturday night was preposterous—Elizabeth returned to the living room. Jasmine was meowing crazily near the door.

Steeling herself, Elizabeth went to the front window and looked outside. The Jeep was gone. *I can't believe it*, she thought, fuming. *Jessica tricked me, and I fell for it!* Elizabeth grabbed the phone and called Lila.

"No, I don't know where Jessica is," Lila said. "But why are you home on Saturday night? Are you and Todd—"

Elizabeth groaned. "Not now, Lila. I'm worried sick about Jessica. She sneaked out while I was in the shower." Lila giggled, and Elizabeth resisted the urge to scream. "Think, Lila! Did Jessica mention any plans she might have had for tonight?"

"No. Sorry, but I have to go, Elizabeth. Bo is on the other line, and we're watching *The Life and Times of François-Noël Babeuf*. It's about a French revolutionist who—"

"I have to find Jessica," Elizabeth interrupted tersely. "Call me if you hear from her."

After Elizabeth hung up, Jasmine jumped into her arms. "What am I going to do with Jessica?" Elizabeth nuzzled the kitten's soft fur, then answered

188

her own question. "I'm going to wring her neck—for starters." Jasmine let out a mournful wail.

Elizabeth forced herself to calm down and think. She'd been under a lot of strain lately, which might explain her sudden panicky feeling. Jessica could have simply gone to the store for ice cream or soda. *But why didn't she tell me or leave a note?* Elizabeth wondered. The icy fear in her gut grew stronger. She was certain that something was terribly wrong.

Her parents were out for the evening, and she didn't want to call them in a state of panic. Elizabeth picked up the phone again and called every girl on the cheerleading squad. But no one knew where Jessica might have gone.

Finally Elizabeth called Todd.

He answered on the second ring. As soon as Elizabeth heard his voice, her eyes filled with tears. "I don't know where Jessica is," she said, sobbing. "I have to find her, but she has the Jeep, and the police found another body, at Secca Lake, and it's a girl with blond hair—"

"I'll be right over," Todd assured her.

Elizabeth took a deep, shaky breath. "Thank you," she replied. But he had already hung up. She wiped her tears with the sleeve of her gray sweater, grateful that Todd was on his way. *Have I been taking his strength and support for granted?* she asked herself. He'd been there for her through so many hardships and understood the way she agonized over Jessica's impulsive pranks.

Elizabeth glanced at the videocassettes on the marble coffee table, the ones she and her sister were supposed to have been watching. *How could you do this to me, Jessica?* she thought.

Jessica drove down Forrest Lane and stopped the Jeep in front of a huge, crumbling old mansion with several towers and gables poking up from its roof. The front yard was overgrown with weeds; the porch sagged to one side. A gnarled old tree stood to the left of the house, its long, crooked branches reaching toward a high window.

A witch's castle? Jessica thought as she stared at the forlorn-looking house. *This can't be where Jonathan lives.* But it was the address Enid had given her and the only house in the area. "This must be it," she said softly. She figured that Jonathan's family was probably in the process of remodeling their home. *I'll bet the inside is much nicer,* she decided hopefully. She took a deep breath and stepped out of the Jeep.

A wispy gray cloud moved across the face of the full moon. The stones in the walkway were cracked and lined with weeds. The place looked positively creepy. Jessica looked around and noticed how desolate the area was.

A gust of wind came up, whipping her hair across her face. Jessica pushed it back and headed toward the front door, undaunted. One of the porch steps had a gaping hole in the center. Jessica narrowly avoided putting her foot right through it. *Nothing will stop me, Jonathan,* she thought with determination.

The sound of her footsteps on the porch seemed unusually loud, as did the beating of her heart. Giddy with anticipation and a twinge of fear, Jessica lifted the brass door knocker.

A million horrible scenarios flashed through Elizabeth's mind as she paced across the living room with Jasmine in her arms. *A girl's body lying in the woods near Secca Lake. . . dead teenagers in Dumpsters . . .*

She heard the sound of a car pulling into the driveway and let out a soft cry of relief. "He's here, Jasmine!" Without bothering to wait for a knock, Elizabeth threw open the front door. "Todd, thank goodness you're here. I've been—" She looked at the guy standing there, and the rest of her sentence faded away. "Joey," she whispered breathlessly.

For a long while neither spoke as they gazed

into each other's eyes. Elizabeth felt a storm of emotions raging through her as she studied the face that had haunted her dreams for so long. His curly light brown hair was somewhat longer than it had been at camp, and he seemed thinner, as if he'd lost weight. But his emerald green eyes and his full red lips were just as she'd remembered. *He's gorgeous!* she thought.

Joey took a step closer. Suddenly they were holding each other in a tight embrace. "I've missed you so much," he whispered against her forehead.

Elizabeth closed her eyes and sighed. She felt as if she'd waited forever for this moment. All of her thoughts and worries—Jessica's disappearance, the dead body at Secca Lake—seemed to float away as Elizabeth gave in to the heavenly joy of being in Joey's arms again.

Todd tapped his fingers on the steering wheel of his BMW as he stared at the red traffic light. "Come on, *change*," he mumbled. Elizabeth had sounded terribly upset over the phone, and he was in a hurry to get to her. He'd rushed out of the house right after her call, leaving a half-eaten bowl of ice cream in his bedroom.

Todd honked impatiently at the car in front of him as soon as the traffic light turned green.

Whether or not Jessica was in trouble, he knew how much Elizabeth worried when she believed her twin was in danger.

He arrived at the Wakefield house a few minutes later and was surprised that Elizabeth wasn't outside. He had expected to see her waiting anxiously for him by the curb. He hopped out of the car and jogged across the lawn.

Todd found the front door slightly ajar. *I wonder what's going on,* he thought, feeling uneasy. He pushed it open—and his heart jumped to his throat. His feet felt as if they were sinking through the floor as he gaped in silent shock at the sight before him.

Elizabeth was in the arms of another guy.

Minutes passed as Jessica stood at the door of the old mansion, waiting for someone to answer. The wind rattled though the sagging porch, shaking the broken shutter on the front window. It blew right through her sheer silk dress. Jessica was freezing.

She lifted the door knocker and banged it firmly several times, then pressed her ear to the door. She couldn't hear any sound coming from inside. "Where are you, Jonathan?" she whispered urgently. Frustrated, Jessica gave the door a good hard kick. *After all the trouble I went through to get out tonight, I can't believe he's not home,* she thought.

Just as she turned to go, the door opened. A strong hand grabbed her arm and pulled her inside.

As Jessica looked up at Jonathan a strange, cold excitement filled her. He was holding a crystal goblet of deep red wine. They were standing in a shadowy foyer; the only source of light was three red candles in a wall sconce behind him. His face was in shadow, but his blue eyes seemed to glow with their own light. Jessica's eyes met his. Without speaking, Jonathan set the wineglass on a side table and turned to her. Her heart hammered against her rib cage in eagerness—and fear. Her breath came in labored gasps, then stopped altogether as he pulled her into his arms. Softly he touched his lips to hers. A small sound of wonder came from Jessica's throat.

Jonathan deepened the kiss, sending sharp tingles up and down her spine. Jessica could almost hear the sound of her blood rushing in her ears like a tidal wave. The kiss went on and on, making her head spin. She felt dizzy and light-headed, as if Jonathan's arms were her only support. Jessica had known that she and Jonathan had something special between them, but the reality surpassed all her dreams.

After several glorious moments of ecstasy,

Jonathan suddenly ended the kiss and pushed her roughly away. Jessica raised her hand to her lips and looked at him with pain and confusion in her eyes.

"You shouldn't have come here, Jessica Wakefield," he whispered. "It may have been the biggest mistake of your life."

*Don't miss Sweet Valley High #127, **Dance of Death,** the second book in this chilling three-part miniseries. Experience the horror lurking in the dark shadows of Sweet Valley!*

SWEET VALLEY HIGH™

Bantam Books in the Sweet Valley High series.

Ask your bookseller for the books you have missed.

SWEET VALLEY HIGH™

THE SADDLE CLUB

by Bonnie Bryant

Saddle up and ride free with Stevie, Carole and Lisa. These three very different girls come together to share their special love of horses and to create The Saddle Club.

Ask your bookseller for any titles you have missed. The Saddle Club series is published by Bantam Books.

THE SADDLE CLUB

Nobody Forgets Their First Love!

Now there's a romance series that gets to the heart of *everyone's* feelings about falling in love. *Love Stories* reveals how boys feel about being in love, too! In every story, a boy and girl experience the real-life ups and downs of being a couple, and share in the thrills, joys, and sorrows of first love.

The Love Stories series is published by Bantam Books.

Available now:

created by Francine Pascal

The *valley* has never been so *sweet*!

Having left Sweet Valley High School behind them, Jessica and Elizabeth Wakefield have begun a new stage in their lives, attending the most popular university around – Sweet Valley University – of course!

Join them and all their friends for fun, frolics and frights on *and* off campus.

Ask your bookseller for any titles you have missed. The Sweet Valley University series is published by Bantam Books.

We hope you enjoyed reading this book. If you would like to receive further information about available titles in the Bantam series, just write to the address below, with your name and address:

KIM PRIOR
Bantam Books
61–63 Uxbridge Road
London W5 5SA

If you live in Australia or New Zealand and would like more information about the series, please write to:

SALLY PORTER
Transworld Publishers (Australia) Pty Ltd
15–25 Helles Avenue
Moorebank
NSW 2170
AUSTRALIA

KIRI MARTIN
Transworld Publishers (NZ) Ltd
3 William Pickering Drive
Albany
Auckland
NEW ZEALAND

All Transworld titles are available by post from:
Bookservice by Post
PO Box 29
Douglas
Isle of Man
IM99 1BQ

Credit Cards accepted.
Please telephone 01624 675137 or fax 01624 670923
or Internet http://www.bookpost.co.uk
or e-mail: bookshop@enterprise.net for details.

Free postage and packing in the UK.
Overseas customers allow £1 per book (paperbacks)
and £3 per book (hardbacks)